TWO SLOUGHS

TWO SLOUGHS

Sally Small

iUniverse, Inc.
New York Bloomington

Two Sloughs

iUniverse books may be ordered through booksellers or by contacting:

iUniverse
1663 Liberty Drive
Bloomington, IN 47403
www.iuniverse.com
1-800-Authors (1-800-288-4677)

ISBN: 978-0-595-52877-6 (pbk)
ISBN: 978-0-595-62932-9 (ebk)

Printed in the United States of America

August

Miss Ruth Hardy eased her car well off the pavement in front of Ike's Cafe. No slack-hipped tomato truck was going to clip her, rattling empty and fast through town on its way back from the cannery. But she was careful not to drive too far onto the shoulder of the levee road. She knew these levee banks along the river, dusty green with cottonwoods and bent willows, ripe with figs and berries and fish guts left by fisherman. These river banks were just piles of sand, broken bricks, wrecked barges, thrown up by Chinamen a century ago to reclaim a swamp. The levees crawled through the Sacramento Delta like worms let out of a bait bucket, forming a thousand scooped out islands of farmland below the level of the river. She knew as well as the next guy that nothing held these levees together except pipe weed and blackberry brambles. What amazed her was how they'd lasted this long.

She was careful about her car because it was brand new, her first since the war, a racy, two-tone green '48 Pontiac, a deluxe coupe, with a lot of get up and go and a cushion on the driver's seat so that she could see out over the wheel. She'd splurged: white wall tires, leatherette upholstery and an a.m. radio. She felt kind of sporty in it. She drove it well, and she drove it fast. But she parked it carefully. Even though she couldn't see them, she knew the men inside Ike's Cafe were all watching. Ruth had been hauled out of ditches in the middle of these Delta islands and pulled out of the mud a couple of times in winter -- mud caked to her high heeled pumps, wheels spinning on the prunings and old planks thrown under her back wheels. She wasn't risking another crack about "women drivers" or, worse, a kindly lecture from some farmer on peat dirt and traction and "flooring it is the <u>worst</u> thing you could do." She looked over her inside shoulder the way her Dad had taught her, backed up a little to straighten the car out, set her hand brake. She left the car windows open, keys in the ignition, her purse on the front seat. Folks around here were offended if you locked your car. And Ike never let her pay for her coffee anyway.

It was a hot August morning in 1948, "after the war." Everybody's life had been framed on one side by the war -- its separations and losses, its relocations and rationings. The children's games, the men's stories, the women's bitter, lonely secrets, all still had their roots in World War II. But now, in August, 1948, the future looked wide open. There was a sense of things starting up again and going sky high.

Ruth put her hands on her round hips and studied Ike's Cafe for a minute or two, squinting nearsightedly, the sun glinting off her thick eyeglasses. She tried to decide whether Ike's had developed any more lean while she was away over the summer. "Cafe" was giving it the benefit of the doubt, she thought. It was a shack, was what it was, slouching in the sun at the east anchorage of the Sacramento River Bridge in the middle of the town of Two Sloughs. A long, sun-bleached wood shack barely wide enough to run a counter the length of it. One window at each end. It was the only building on the "river side" of the River Road and it seemed to be attached to the levee by the wild blackberry vines that nearly overran it. The back end of Ike's Café shambled out over the river on wood stilts that rotted and collapsed every few years. At the far end of the counter the linoleum floor slumped. Ruth always avoided the stools at that far end if she could help it. There was a sign nailed up out front above the window, but it had blistered so that only the I was clearly legible. Everybody on the river knew Ike anyway, knew it was Ike's Cafe.

She could see Ike through the rusted screen door, standing over his well-greased griddle, scraping the griddle from right to left so that he formed a kind of levee of his own, composed of the remains of the day's breakfast orders, along the left edge. The smell of frying bacon floated right out the door to greet her. The farmers at the counter had been up since 4:30 a.m. When they came into Ike's for breakfast, they had built up an appetite. A mound of hash browns rested in the back corner of his griddle. A wire basket of eggs sat beside it -- eggs with deep yellow yolks that Ike fried so the yolks were runny, and the whites were crisp around the edges. Ruth watched him flip three pancakes, crack two eggs onto the hot surface, turn to wipe the counter with a piece of old towel. Bacon grease splattered the wide front of his apron. Ike was an extra helping of a man, ample, with a big, bald head and a lop-sided grin, as if the joke were just between the two of you. He wore a pencil behind his ear, but Ruth guessed it must be decoration for his bald head. She'd never seen him use it. People said what they wanted and then left what they knew they owed on the counter.

It was 10:00 o'clock. Ruth Hardy could have told the time without looking at her watch by the population on the stools and the number of pickups out front. Two Sloughs was an unincorporated town, but that didn't mean it lacked organization. You just had to know where to look for it. Ruth knew that every morning an informal town meeting was held at Ike's: all white; all male. Minutes of the meeting went something like this:

"Bud."

"Ike."

"Jus' coffee. Maybe one of them glazed...."

Ike talked with his hands, spatula in one hand, coffeepot in the other: "See you're picking out on Dead Horse, Harvey." Ike pointed East toward Dead Horse Island with his spatula hand.

"Yup. Too damn green, though."

"Well, with this weather..."

And then they'd talk about the weather, the way farmers do, earnestly, because it mattered. City folks used the weather as polite opening chitchat, but for these farmers it was their life, hinged to ripeness and harvest and rot.

By noon all the news of Two Sloughs would have been spread around. Problems would have been addressed or sympathetically avoided. Plans would have been made. Ruth had seen it happen. All without one of these weary men hunched at the counter uttering more than six words in a row. They sat face forward, forearms heavy on the counter, as she saw them now, shirts already stuck to their backs in the heat, forearms tanned - a farmer's tan - tanned up to their elbows, backs of their necks and ears burnt red. Their hats hung behind them on hooks -- John Deere tractor caps, narrow brimmed Stetsons with sweat-stained bands. They knew each other two, sometimes three generations deep. They knew the son who was farming because his older brother, his father's favorite, had been lost on Guadalcanal. They knew the young man who was having trouble with his restless, city-born wife; the old man who was brooding over his grandchild's polio. This abiding knowledge gave the kidding, the conversation, the long silences all equal weight.

"Louie, you hear about this corn growing contest?"

"You oughta enter, Louie. You could win'er easy."

"It's a big, national, god-damned deal, Louie. You could...."

Ruth felt an almost imperceptible break in the conversation when she let the screen door slam behind her. She was the only woman in the place.

"Ruth."

"Ike."

"Coffee?" Ike was already filling the thick white mug, leaving room for cream, because he knew she took cream.

Now, Ruth occupied a special position in Two Sloughs, and the town took care of her. She was only thirty-four, but she'd been principal of the Two Sloughs Elementary School for eight years now, and there wasn't a better Elementary School in the state. She was young for a principal. She'd come to Two Sloughs straight out of college to teach fourth grade. Two years later the principal had joined up, and it was catch as catch can. The school board had been nervous about it, but they'd given her the job. She'd proven to be tough as an old boot. She'd had run-ins with nearly every seventh grade boy in Two Sloughs, and most of their mothers, too. Every man in Ike's admired her a lot, feared her a little. Their wives all thought they should find Ruth a husband. "She could use a husband," was how they put it; she was past thirty. The men all agreed, but to tell the truth, they couldn't see it. Ruth was about five feet tall, and sturdily built, like a corn silo, like a Sherman tank. She had thin, light brown curly hair with a mind of its own. Sometimes it looked like the coat on a wet cocker spaniel; sometimes it looked like a dandelion gone to seed. Her coke bottle glasses made her round blue eyes pounce out at you. Her voice had some grit to it.

She wore tailored dresses, brown, printed with little white sprigs of something, and high heels so that she didn't have to look up to the eighth grade boys. She wore her high heels out on the football field where she coached boys' football. Well, somebody had to do it. The men had been away. She wore her high heels on the baseball diamond where she coached the softball teams, took batting practice. When she connected, look out. If they'd ever gotten around to building her a fence out there, she'd have cleared it four out of five times.

She wore those high heels at band practice, where she directed the band and taught all the instruments. And at chorus, which she also conducted. She had the ankles for shoes like that -- solid. Every single student over the fourth grade had to be in the school band or Miss Hardy couldn't field a band large enough to qualify for the state competition. The same was true of the chorus. If a child was tone deaf, he played the cymbals. The most hopeless cases played the triangle. Some years the percussion section got pretty cumbersome.

Miss Ruth Hardy's theory on education was simple: You could learn anything if you worked hard enough at it. Her theory on discipline was equally direct: If you deserved it, you got it. Many irate fathers and tearful mothers had sat in Miss Hardy's dark, cluttered office and heard these philosophies briefly expounded. Ruth Hardy only came to Ike's when she needed something. The men cradled their coffee mugs and waited to hear what it was.

Ruth hitched herself up onto a stool between Dan Martin and Louie Riccetti.

"Back to work, Ruth?" Dan Martin turned to her and smiled. His thick shock of blonde hair stuck out sideways, like wheat hit by a hailstorm. All his features clustered in the center of his broad, sunburned face. Rivulets of sweat streaked the dirt on the sides of his cheeks. She had picked the stool next to him on purpose.

"That time of year," Ruth said. Her voice sounded gruff with the embarrassment she always felt coming to Ike's. Partly it was the clubbiness of the place; partly it was because she did only come when she had a favor to ask. She glanced sideways down the row of faces, took a sip of her coffee, tried again. "It's gonna be a scorcher today." She turned to Dan, "You figure to pick through September?"

"If the weather holds. Maybe longer."

"Looks like we'll have more migrant kids than usual then."

"Could be."

"Think we could round up some shoes?"

"Huh?"

"It's the darned State," Ruth said apologetically. "These Okie kids never have shoes. The State says kids have to wear shoes to go to school - some health code thing. Or else they're afraid all this education will leak out through the soles of their feet. Anyway, I'd like to get them fitted with a pair before they take off down the valley, and the weather turns cold." She added cream to her coffee from the metal pitcher, took a sip. "Also it's a good bribe to get their parents to send them to school. I don't have to go out after them this way." She concentrated on her coffee mug.

This was a trump card, and she knew it. The men shifted on their stools, stared into their coffee cups, remembering the time Ruth went out to one of the migrant camps after some kids who weren't coming to school. The father had leaned out a window and tried to scare her off with a shotgun. When that hadn't worked, he'd stomped out onto the front stoop of that ramshackle house and shot a hole in her tire as she stood in the weeds beside the car.

Ruth remembered it, too. Nobody'd ever shot at Ruth before. It scared her so badly she nearly wet her pants. She couldn't believe it. She stood staring down at her shredded tire, thinking this can't be happening. And then she got mad. She knew if she let this Okie run her off, she'd never see another migrant kid in Two Sloughs Elementary. She pulled her tire iron out of her trunk and told him to change that tire and put those kids in the back seat of her car or they'd end up just like him, broke and always having to move on and never to anything better. She was getting red in the face even thinking about it: she, standing in the weeds, brandishing that tire iron, locking her knees so her legs wouldn't shake, squinting into the sun; the father, thin as a stalk, unshaven, his face in shadow, glowering at her over the barrel of his gun, a meanness in him learned the hard way. She told him his kids were smart, trying to gentle her voice a little. She told him his daughter was good at arithmetic, real good; that the little one, Tommy, was the best reader in the first grade. But they wouldn't stand a chance without school. She told him that just because he'd missed out didn't mean his kids had to. "Here," she said, offering him the tire iron again. "Do it for your kids."

What was she thinking? Lucky she hadn't gotten herself killed. She drove out there and picked those kids up every day for two weeks until the story got around, and somebody who lived out that way offered to bring them in. The funny thing was those kids had come back every year after that, the Weaver kids, were still coming.

"Ruth, do us a favor, don't go out hunting any more Okies. What size shoes you want?"

"Oh, assorted," Ruth said breezily. She had no idea what would turn up the first day of school. "And maybe some clean T-shirts?"

"Next week soon enough?"

"That'd be fine." She picked up her coffee mug with both hands and took another long sip. The walls of Ike's were glazed the color of the oil in the deep fat fryer. A pinup calendar hung on the wall. This month's pouty calendar girl spilled out of an abbreviated sailor suit. She held a length of rope as if she had no idea in the world what to do with it, and she was so splattered with bacon grease that parts of her anatomy were nearly transparent. To her embarrassment, Ruth often found herself seated smack in front of the calendar, so that when she looked up from her coffee, she confronted the ample, pink buttocks of Miss July or the overflowing bosom of Miss September. Were there really women who looked like that? The calendar girls made Ruth feel uncomfortably drab. Beside the calendar hung a sign board with the menu and prices slid into the grooves, letter by letter and number by number. But it provided no distraction. It featured MEATLOA and EEF STEW, neither of which had been available at Ike's ever, as far as Ruth could tell. The prices on the signboard had numbers missing, too. But everybody knew. Coffee was a nickel, all you could drink. Bacon and eggs were 35 cents. For lunch you had your choice: hamburger, tuna or egg. The bread was white. The lettuce was wilted. You got a slice of tomato during tomato season if somebody remembered to drop off a lug. Same with onions. For dessert there were jars of peanut butter and apricot jam on the counter, bread in baskets. Help yourself.

"Anybody know how to fix a lawn mower?" Ruth asked.

Any place else, all eyes would have turned toward Ben Heimann, but in Two Sloughs men didn't do that. They all waited for Ben to say something.

"Bad gas again?" Ben asked.

"I don't think so, Ben. I filled it myself, used the formula you gave me. There doesn't seem to be any spark at all."

"I better pick it up then. You gonna be around later?"

"Thanks Ben." Ruth drained her coffee mug, looked longingly at the glazed doughnuts in the glass case, then at the calendar girl. She needed to watch her weight. "Thanks, Ike." She walked out, and the screen door slammed behind her.

The men at the counter watched her walk out to her car, watched her drive off, made a mental note to tell her that her right rear tire looked low.

"You want the shoes at your place, Dan, or at school?"

"Thanks, Louie. My place 'd be fine. Don't leave them on the porch, though. Kids got a new puppy. Chews up everything."

"Lord knows, the boys grow out of 'em fast enough. We ought to have some around."

"Yeah, I'll ask Charlene."

"I hope she was listening to you, though," Freddy said. "She scares me sometimes."

Dan chuckled and pushed his mug forward for a refill. Freddy Noble was the mildest man in town, a harmonica player, a widower. "She scares us all, Freddy. She scares us all."

Freddy shook his head and smiled, "She wants all the first graders vaccinated again. Right away, while the migrants are still around." Freddy was the town pharmacist, proprietor of the Two Sloughs Pharmacy and Soda Fountain. "Think if I could get the vaccine at cost the Rotary Club might pop?" Freddy asked of no one in particular. "Maybe a hundred bucks, maybe less. She'll talk Doc and Mabel into going over again and giving the shots for free, I imagine."

Bill Pratt leaned forward on the counter. "She's already hit me up for it," he said. "Told me $50. Said if Rotary didn't come up with it, she'd steal it out of the milk money."

"She would, too." Louie said.

"She <u>could</u>," Dan said, laughing. "Ping Lowe told me she had conned him into giving her the school milk at half price. His patriotic duty, she told him."

"Ought to find that woman a husband," said Harvey.

Everybody chuckled, then lapsed into one last, easy silence. They all had to get back to work. Ruth Hardy was right. It was going to be a scorcher, and they all knew it. They sat heavily on their stools, enjoying for a minute just sitting there.

Ruth drove away feeling unaccountably lighthearted. They were good men, tired but good. Her school year was the reverse of the farming calendar. As she got started, full of vinegar and new ideas, the farmers were finishing up their harvests. By late August she could almost see the haze of exhaustion that hung over the men and women of Two Sloughs, the combined effect of long hot days, too little sleep and too much riding on getting the crops in all at once; the pears ripening too fast, then the tomatoes, a drizzle of rain at the wrong time, then the corn, and finally the sugar beets. She had heard it in the weary voices at Ike's, seen how they kind of bluffed their way through the oppressive heat of August with the shoelaces of their boots broken and knotted, their knuckles scraped, the dusty dashboards of their pickups littered with baling wire and Band-Aid boxes.

She had to be careful how much she asked of them at the beginning of the school year. After the rains settled in, October maybe, everybody relaxed some. They'd either made it or they hadn't, depending on the pear price or the tomato price or some price they wouldn't know 'til long after they'd finished picking. They'd start out next year owing the bank a little less or a little more; that was all. Ruth could count on help for the Christmas program. But now, at the end of August, she had to watch it.

She drove along the levee road, past the businesses perched along the levee, all in a row on the inland side. Only Ike's hung longways, precariously, on the river side of the road. Most of the riverbank was choked with wild grape and blackberry, shaded by huge cottonwoods that leaned over the river. A good town, she thought. She passed the Two Sloughs Pharmacy; the Bank of Thurgood Bream with its preposterous Ionic columns. She stopped at the Post Office to pick up the school mail. She said hello to Elsie, the postmistress, asked after her mother, heard that another crop duster had tried to duck under another power line and killed himself, and picked up her summer mail. Elsie was busy, but Ruth did get the current number of General Deliveries at the Post Office, so that she and Elsie could make a rough estimate of the number of migrant families in town. Coming out of the Post Office, she could see a gang of children inside the door of Ping Lowe's Grocery, jiggling the gum ball machine, sprawling on the wood floor reading comic books. Time for school, all right. Clarence Henderson said, "Hi, Ruth," and did she know her right rear tire looked kinda' low. A small town, she thought, getting back in her car, a town where everybody minded everybody else's business. A great place to raise children. Harder to survive as an adult.

The town had a name, Two Sloughs, but Ruth had noticed that nobody used it much. The sloughs led off into narrow waterways, sunken islands and tule swamps choked with water lily, tangled in grape and blackberry vines, known only to the beaver trappers and bass fishermen. People just said, "The River." The Sacramento River snaked through the farmland the full length of the Sacramento Valley. Only the flimsy network of islands and levees held the river back from sprawling out over the vast alluvial plain that formed the center of California. Pot-bellied tug boats hauled barges bulging with oil and grain and gravel up and down the Sacramento River from San Francisco to Sacramento, blowing three long blasts on their horns to open up the Two Sloughs drawbridge. All directions were calculated by the river: "up the river about a mile," people told her, or, "down the river toward Andrus Island," "across the river." But those directions discounted the twists and turns the river took, the sloughs that cut in. For the first two years she lived in Two Sloughs, she was lost half of the time.

The Chinese lived "up the river" in an old and separate community left over from the levee building in the 1800s. "Across the river" the "whites," a loose assortment of Portuguese, Irish and Ruth had no idea what all, had turned a worn-out asparagus field into "Lambert Tract," three blocks of wood frame houses with front porches, cement walks and square patches of Bermuda grass lawn, propped up by a pink stucco Catholic church on one side, and a gray clapboard Presbyterian church on the other. A small town. Ruth smiled to herself, but diverse, God knows. The population of the town was only 750, but it had segregated itself into various pockets and neighborhoods. Most of the farmers still lived scattered on the land they farmed. The Filipinos were mostly bachelors and lived on the ranches.

Ruth drove down off the levee into Japan Town, waved at Mrs. Kobayashi out on her unpainted back porch, and Mrs. Kobayashi waved her dented tin colander in return. Mrs. Kobayashi grew bean sprouts and made bean curd for the Japanese community of Two Sloughs. Her screened porch was as damp and spongy as a swamp from her constant watering and washing. She wore a rubber apron, green rubber boots and rubber gloves, so the children in town called her Frog Lady. Beside her porch she grew tall rows of slender Japanese leeks.

Ruth pulled up in front of the Two Sloughs Elementary School, a low stucco building built down off the levee, beside the Japanese community, a quarter mile or so from Ike's Cafe and the Two Sloughs Bridge.   A flagpole and a clump of ragged redwood trees stood sentinel out front. Planted by the Class of 1907 to commemorate Luther Burbank's visit to Two Sloughs, the redwoods had survived Boy Scout hatchets and tree climbing contests. Spindly trees, planted every year on Luther Burbank's birthday, surrounded the school's dirt playing fields. Apparently, Luther Burbank was the only famous man ever to visit Two Sloughs, and the town hadn't gotten over it. The school wasn't much to look at, but it was what she had, and it was clean, or would be when Mr. Mundorf got through with it. Mr. Mundorf had been badly wounded in the first war. He was stooped and disfigured and blind in one eye, but he was thorough, a worthy adversary to the peat dirt that sifted in through every window crack when the north wind blew and the tule mud that caked the kids' shoes all winter.

Ruth let herself in the front door of the empty school. The teachers wouldn't be back until next week. The hallways were cool and dark. She went into her office without turning on any lights, settled into the oak swivel chair behind her desk, kicked off her high-heeled pumps and leaned back. Her summer had been hectic. She'd gone to stay with her younger sister Jean in Oregon. Jeanie was recovering from a botched hysterectomy, a mess of a marriage, too, in Ruth's opinion, and three small children too close together, who ran wild. Jean's husband had been off at a logging camp most of the summer, so Ruth had tried to nurse Jean, paint the kitchen and keep the dog hair and the sour diaper pail under control, but it was discouraging business. The memory of their mother's disappointment in Jean bit at them both all summer. The "I told you sos" hung over Jeanie's life like the cloud of mosquitoes outside the screen door.

Elizabeth Hardy, Ruth's mother, had been a thin little wren of a woman with busy, fidgety hands that picked at lint off the girls' sweaters, drummed time on the piano bench, pushed the girls' hair back out of their eyes. An intelligent, musical woman, she'd "thrown her life away" by marrying her high school sweetheart and having two babies before she could turn around. She never got an education and never forgave herself for it. It frustrated her that her husband, Ruth's father, who had had two years of college before he went into the navy, hadn't made more of himself. Fiercely ambitious for her two daughters, she drilled into the girls' heads that they must graduate from college at the same time she drilled them in their piano scales and their spelling lists. Elizabeth Hardy hadn't lived to see Jeanie marry the fullback on the Cal football team the summer after her freshman year. Ruth half suspected her mother of dying to avoid attending the wedding.

One morning this summer in her sister Jeanie's Oregon kitchen, Jeanie had turned on Ruth, "You always were perfect."

"Jeanie, don't even start that."

"It wasn't any trouble for you. You never liked men...."

"Jeanie...."

"Al said right off you were frigid. He said men could tell." Ruth had clenched the worn-out dish brush, leaned against the sink, clamped her mouth shut. Even as a kid, when she was hurt, Jeanie had lashed back with her tongue, that barbed tongue of hers. Ruth had always thought of it as a fish hook tongue. It bit into you, sank deep, worked its way deeper. Ruth had tended to fight with her fists, to kick or bite, but Jeanie had learned to inflict the deeper wounds.

This time it was Jeanie who had ended up sobbing, sprawled in a wobbly, wired-together kitchen chair. Her faded pink chenille bathrobe flapped open revealing a too sheer, discolored nightgown with fragments of torn lace around the hem. The lace had come unstitched from the nightgown so that it hung in ragged scallops around Jeanie's knees.

Ruth stroked her sister's knee, let her cry. "Sis, it's just a lot harder time for you right now than it is for me. I'll get my turn, and you'll have to come rescue me."

"Is that how you see it? Rescuing?"

Ruth looked at her sister's puffy tear-streaked face. Jeanie's face was the color of crab meat, she thought, white, mottled, bluish around the eyelids. Ruth shook her head and laughed in spite of herself, "Well, drowning in a diaper pail would be an awful way to go. Come on, Jeanie. To hell with the kitchen. Let's take the kids and go to the beach."

Any way Ruth looked at it, it had been a long, backbreaking summer. She nearly cried for joy when she came back to her neat, quiet bungalow outside of Two Sloughs with her Shasta daisies in the backyard. She had a stack of paperwork to do, and she must do it or the District wouldn't give her the money she needed. But for the moment she simply sat, enjoying the silence, the order, the smell of Mr. Mundorf's paste wax and varnish.

The more she saw of marriage, the more it troubled her. Her sister Jeanie wasn't just sick, she was despondent, overwhelmed by her children and her churlish husband. Ruth saw it again and again in Two Sloughs -- perky young women, who gradually sank beneath the weight of poverty, and too much washing, the heat and the dust in summer, the tule fog and the mud in winter; pretty young women whose hair turned lank, whose shoulders rounded in defeat. Her own parents' marriage had been a mare's nest. Her mother was devoted to her father, strove savagely to improve him. Her father sympathized with her mother's disappointment in him, but he remained fondly, cheerfully unrepentant.   Ruth and her sister grew up seesawing between them, intrigued by their mother's horrible predictions, lured by their father's rosy promises.   It was a happy childhood.   But there was an edge to it.   The girls were occasionally knocked off balance by the truth, which caught them unawares, tangled as it was in their parents' marital struggles: The longed-for trips to San Francisco that were planned and promised and then called off at the last minute, the singing lessons that had to be given up suddenly mid-year, the college tuition money that never materialized.

She knew Two Sloughs thought she was an old maid. "What that woman needs is a husband," the men said behind her back, meaning a man tough enough to make her heel.   They might have been talking about one of their best hunting bitches.   The women said "We have to find a man for Ruth," as if they'd been sorting socks and had noticed a stray sock without its mate. What Ruth felt at the moment was darned fortunate.

She stretched out luxuriously in her office chair, swiveled.   Mr. Mundorf had oiled her chair, varnished her oak desk and file cabinet over the summer, and washed the Venetian blinds.   Reams of new mimeograph paper were stacked   neatly   beside   the   mimeograph   machine.   Her   Noah   Adams Lumberyard calendar had been turned to the month of September.   The whole year lay ahead of her.

The sharp ping of a BB against the window broke her reverie.   She looked through her Venetian blinds out onto the playground.   Two sixth graders lay on their bellies next to the basketball standard.   One of them aimed a BB gun directly at her office.   Ping.   The boys looked up and laughed.   They seemed to have hit the bull's eye.   Ruth strode down the hall and out onto the playground, surprising the two gunmen, who looked up as if a ghost of school past had suddenly appeared beside them.

"Give me that thing, Lionel."

"School isn't in yet."

"Lionel!" Ruth reached out.

"Honest, Miss Hardy, we didn't know you were around," Jimmy Martin gasped as he scrambled to his feet.

Lionel Noble bit his lip and reluctantly put the BB gun into Miss Hardy's outstretched hand.

"Lionel, you were aiming at the windows in my office."

A wicked glimmer caught in Lionel's hazel eyes.   His shaggy red hair stood on end.   His freckles had multiplied over the summer and his lashes had turned blond so that he resembled some wild Appaloosa pony now, standing captured but defiant before her.

"If Mr. Mundorf had been in there cleaning, you could have put out his only good eye. You don't point this thing at <u>anybody</u>. Do you understand me?"

Lionel matched her, angry stare for angry stare, outrage for outrage. The ripe August sun beat on the school yard; the asphalt oozed around their feet. This kid never backed down. Every school, every town, has a Lionel, Ruth thought, a kid who attracts trouble, a captivating kid with a mean streak in him. A wake of blown-up tool sheds and tortured cats lay in Lionel's eleven-year-old path. God only knew what lay ahead.

"Jimmy, you go home and tell your mother you stay after school the whole first week. Lionel, you come with me."

"What did <u>he</u> do? He didn't do nothing." Lionel demanded.

"He didn't do <u>anything</u>," corrected Miss Hardy. "He should have hit you over the head with a brick."

Miss Hardy turned on her heels and headed for her office carrying the BB gun. She could hear Lionel scuffing along behind her. Lionel Noble drove her crazy. He was the one kid in school she couldn't get through to. She couldn't encourage him; she couldn't outwit him; she couldn't even cow him, and, Heaven help her, she'd tried. How Freddy Noble, the sweetest guy in town, could have spawned this wild pony, hell-colt of a child, she couldn't imagine. He didn't even look like Freddy, who was small and slender with obedient brown hair and poetic, near-sighted brown eyes. Apparently Lionel took after his fierce Irish mother, who drove into the river when Lionel was four, leaving Freddy to cope with this flaming boy child.

Ruth led the way into the school building, cool and dark after the heat of the playground. She couldn't count the times she had called Freddy into her office or he had called her late at night to talk about Lionel. Freddy was at his wit's end. And so was she.

"He's so angry," Freddy would say sadly. "Why's he so angry at me? I didn't take his mother away from him. God did."

Which was why Freddy had tried Sunday School for Lionel, but Lionel had put mice in Retta Mae Henderson's piano bench. When Retta Mae sat down to play "Onward Christian Soldiers" and then opened the piano bench to investigate the scratching sounds beneath her, Lionel was pretty much given his marching orders. Pastor Rehmke said that Lionel had been given to the Presbyterians by God, "To test us," he said.

But Retta Mae said he hadn't been given to <u>her</u>, thank God, and she wasn't having him in her Sunday school class. Period. "It's too late for Sunday School for Lionel," she said. "You should have started him at an earlier age."

Ruth turned the light on in her office, firmly deposited the BB gun in the closet and locked the closet door. She was playing for time, and she had the irritating suspicion that Lionel knew she was playing for time. She sat down behind her desk. Lionel skulked behind the two parents' conference chairs.

Freddy signed Lionel up for Cub Scouts the day he turned seven. Lionel set fire to Harvey Lemmon's barley field on the first troop hike. The fire might have been an accident, but when one of the Den Mothers found a gopher snake wrapped up in a hot dog bun on the first troop cookout, Lionel was through.

"What am I going to do with you, Lionel? School hasn't even started, and already you've wound up in my office."

Lionel grinned. His grin had gotten him into almost as much trouble as his bad deeds. An unrepentant ear-to-ear grin. It bewitched his peers and caused panic among his superiors. Ruth had never run into a child so resistant to her methods. She prided herself on being a pretty good educator, but Lionel seemed to be unreachable. And he seemed to take pleasure in making a fool out of her.

"I'll have to call your father and tell him about this," she said.

A cloud passed over Lionel's face. Freddy wasn't firm enough with the boy. The whole town concurred in this opinion. But the boy adored his father. The one time Ruth had seen Lionel's wicked grin shatter was when Doc Graham came to school last winter to tell Lionel that he'd taken Freddy to the hospital in Sacramento. Freddy had developed pneumonia, and Doc Graham wanted him in the hospital for a couple of days. Lionel turned ash gray at the news and burst into tears in Ruth's office. Finally Ruth agreed to take him up to the hospital after school. Once he got there, he refused to leave his father's bedside until his dad was released two days later. At Ruth's suggestion, Doc put Freddy under Lionel's care for a week. Ruth brought Lionel's homework every night, and the neighbors dropped off dinners. Even Doc had to admit that Lionel had been a model nurse. And Lionel's homework had never been done better.

Every evening of that wintry week Ruth sat with Lionel at a card table in Freddy's bedroom checking Lionel's homework in low voices so that Freddy could doze. Ruth remembered those nights. The room was an odd combination of faded feminine touches and utilitarian additions. Limp organdy curtains hung in the windows, a worn yellow chintz chair stood in the corner. It must have matched the headboard at one time and possibly a bedspread. Probably it had been a cheerful, sunny room, facing east. Now it looked wan, diluted by old quilts and spare army blankets, crowded with card tables and stacks of books beside the bed. Ruth was embarrassed to be forced into such an intimate glimpse of Freddy Noble's life, but Lionel wouldn't budge from the room. And Freddy, lying weakly against his pillows seemed pleased to see them working at the card table under the light of the floor lamp. Ruth had felt him smiling at them as they sat bent over Lionel's arithmetic problems.

Lionel did good work that week, and Ruth had praised him for it. Maybe this is what Lionel needed, Ruth had thought, a good dose of responsibility. Doc Graham had been tough on the kid. He made him keep charts of Freddy's temperature, how many glasses of water he drank. Doc made Lionel change the pillow slips every day. Lionel asked Ruth to check his charts, too, along with his homework, before he gave them to Doc Graham.

But Freddy recovered, and two weeks after Lionel was back in school, Mrs. McClatchy opened her bottom desk drawer to find a dead lizard draped around her prized alligator handbag.

Ruth straightened the pile of mail on her desk blotter and waited for Lionel to look up. She had to say something. He'd caught her unprepared. School didn't start for a week. "Your father isn't going to like this," she said.

There was a long silence. Lionel studied the laces of his high tops. "O.K.," Lionel said, finally, "I'll take trombone."

"What?" But Ruth understood immediately what Lionel was saying to her: If she didn't tell his father about the BB gun, Lionel would agree to play trombone in the school band. Ruth caught herself before she smiled at the ingenuity of Lionel's scheme. The instrument case for the trombone was heavy and hard to carry home. Nobody liked to take trombone. She always had trouble filling the trombone section. This squirt was attempting to bribe her.

"No deal, Lionel. I'm not sure I'd risk putting a trombone in your hands anyway. It makes too much noise. I'm going to tell your father that the BB gun stays locked in my closet for one month. If you can keep out of trouble for one month, you'll get it back." Ruth tried to read the freckled face before her, but Lionel stood wriggling his toes inside his high tops, staring at his shoes. Ruth sighed. "I'll let you out the front door," she said.

Ruth watched him from the window. Half way down the front steps Lionel stopped, wheeled around and flashed Ruth a look of 99 proof hate. Then he leapt into the air, skipped the last two steps and dashed off.

Well, she hadn't been ready for that one. She'd handled it all wrong. She should have.... What? School wasn't even in session yet, and she and Lionel were at each other's throats.

That evening was warm and still, Obon weather, the August monsoon festival for the Japanese Buddhist community, although in Two Sloughs it hadn't rained since April and wasn't likely to rain again until October. Ruth slathered on her mosquito repellent and drove to Japan Town. After all, every Japanese parent came faithfully to her band concerts, chorus programs and operettas. It seemed to Ruth the least she could do. The Japanese women practiced for Obon weeks beforehand. Mrs. Nakamura had given Ruth a blue and white cotton kimono that she loved and had encouraged Ruth to learn the dances. But Ruth balked, too embarrassed to try. The Japanese women were all slender and graceful. Ruth felt like a chunk of cheese beside them.

There were several guests this year. She recognized their cars parked in front of Japanese School. Next door, on the porch of the Buddhist temple, the long dark konsho bell hunched motionless. Ruth passed the two bonsaied pine trees that flanked the temple steps, ("Hell of a way to prune a tree," the farmers always said when they saw them.) She walked out onto the freshly mown field beside the temple. A tangle of electric wires strung loosely in the air from bamboo poles formed a spidery circle, and a collection of mismatched paper lanterns swayed from the drooping electric wires: round pink lanterns with flowers printed on them, a small green lantern, three white lanterns with "Kikoman Soy Sauce" printed on their pleated shades.... Then, as Ruth approached the circle of dangling lanterns, the electricity went on, and all the lanterns glowed golden. Smoke from the burning stubble fields behind them lingered in the air, softening the scene, giving it the faded, other-worldly look of a woodblock print on rice paper. Moths began to flutter in the lantern light.

Ruth loved Obon. The Japanese families seemed so at home in this festival. It enjoyed the warmth and informality of summertime. It was held outdoors, young and old participated, the traditions seemed simple, the mood quiet. Shiz Ota came up to Ruth and gave her a hug. "I was afraid you weren't back yet. And you wore your kimono. June will be happy. Here, take my fan. It's hot." She handed Ruth her round paper fan with a stick handle. Ruth was wishing she hadn't worn her kimono. She flapped the fan Shiz had given her. She felt like a fool. She hadn't known anybody outside the Japanese community would be at the dances. Usually she simply sat with the grandmothers and nodded and smiled.

Three musicians had already taken their places on planks elevated by lug boxes in the middle of the grassy clearing, and the dancers were forming a big circle around them under the lanterns. Shiz went to join in. Tosh Nakamura, unofficial head of the Japanese community, bowed to Ruth, welcomed her. He led her to one of the folding chairs set up outside the circle, next to Doc

Graham, his wife Caroline and Freddy Noble, the pharmacist. Ruth was politely offered rice balls, which she loved, and sake, which she hated but took. Then Tosh returned to the center of the circle to begin the dances.

"Nice to see you Ruth. Pleasant summer with your sister?" Caroline Graham asked in her gentle southern drawl. Caroline looked slim and cool in her pink linen sheath. Ruth felt hot and dumpy, dolled up in her kimono, which she now realized she had folded backwards across her chest, right over left, not left over right, as Mrs. Nakamura had instructed her. Right over left was for dressing corpses. Mrs. Nakamura had been fussy about that. Ruth fanned her cheeks.

"It was just about enough motherhood for me, Caroline," she said testily. "I'll admit I was glad to get home. And you? Good summer?"

"Oh, it was just about enough Two Sloughs for me," Caroline said sarcastically. "A couple of wheat fields burned up. Marietta Heimann was crowned queen of The Bass Derby. That was the main cultural event."

Ruth didn't touch it. Caroline was from Charleston, South Carolina, which, she reminded anybody who would listen, was culturally superior to Two Sloughs.

A cluster of old ladies sat on the other side of Ruth chattering in Japanese. They bowed and smiled at her, then turned to greet nephews and nieces as they arrived from Sacramento and stopped to say hello before joining the circle. The Sacramentans wore sports clothes and sandals, but once the dances started they fell into line, remembering the steps, watching Tosh.

The Nisei children glanced shyly sideways at Ruth from under their straight bangs as they danced by in the circle, following their mothers. Most of the girls wore kimonos. The boys wore square cut jackets and cotton sashes around their heads that slipped rakishly over their eyebrows. Nearly half the students in Ruth's school were the children of this community, and Ruth struggled to come up with names after a summer's absence and two inches' growth. There was also the mind-boggling names confusion: half the children were named Toshiko or Shizue or some traditional name; the other half were named Lorraine or Ronald or Roy. She began to feel slightly cross-eyed as they all moved past, taller and skinnier and missing more teeth.

The musicians took a break. The circle reversed. Tosh put a record on the record player. Now the women followed Kimi Sugimoto in a special dance that they had just learned. This year many of them wore pale blue cotton kimonos figured with a trailing white wisteria pattern. Their feet were clad in elegant white tabis. They clapped their hands together palm to palm. Ruth watched as they pattered around the circle to the scratchy music of the high, haunting song. But it was their arms and their fingers, sweeping out of their wide-winged kimono sleeves that seemed to Ruth to do the dancing.

Ruth watched Shiz as her arms wove in and out of the circle, as graceful as flight. Her fingertips swayed delicately upwards, like feathers, a slender, feminine grace that seemed nearly magical to Ruth.

Ruth had been her father's only son. She'd learned to hit a sinking fastball, throw a football in a spiral, learned to shoot straight and cast a fishing line half way across the river. She'd been her mother's hope for academic achievement. Feminine grace had been Jeanie's department, a sort of consolation prize for not being good at school. In any case, Ruth wasn't mentally or physically suited to slender delicacy. She just loved to watch it. Maybe she really wasn't very feminine, she mused, as she watched the women dance. Maybe she was too chunky, too cold, too tough. These women looked as if they <u>were</u> wisteria vines as they swayed to the music of the stringed koto, these women who stood twelve hours a day in suffocating canneries and packing sheds, dizzy from the sorting belts, sick from the heat, these women who had been rooted out of town at the start of the war, with cardboard tags tied around their necks, Shiz had told her, "no name; only a number, as if we were for sale." These women who had been forced to stuff their own straw mattresses, to live in horse stalls, "a wretched place, the wind, the stench of horse urine." Shiz said she had come back after the war and found that somebody had broken into the shed where their household goods were stored and smashed every piece of furniture, ripped up every family photograph, unpacked every piece of china and thrown it against the wall. These women possessed a liquid femininity that Ruth could never dream of having herself. Ruth was feeling downright claustrophobic in her kimono. She gave her fan another swat. She was here as the principal of the local school, for crying out loud. She'd better pull herself together.

In most aspects of the life of Two Sloughs the Japanese families remained polite but completely separate. The old men seemed to Ruth particularly distant, almost ghost-like, as if they had had their identities confiscated in the internment camps and had never been able to regain them. ("The shame of it for my father," Shiz said. "He was a citizen.") Tosh never went to Ike's for coffee, for instance, wouldn't have felt welcome. Ben Heimann had lost a son on Guam. Thurgood Bream's grandson went down in the Coral Sea. There were still hard feelings around town. They attended their own church, took care of their own community's drunks and widows. The men stood off to the side even now, arms crossed, while the women danced.

But where school was concerned, the Japanese community was fully engaged. Ruth had never seen anything like it. School segregation had ended for their children the year Ruth began teaching, and the Japanese parents had been adamant about education ever since. The children arrived clean and pressed, promptly, with their faces quietly composed. They were as full of mischief as the other children, but where the white faces were as mobile as bubble gum, the Japanese faces were capable of great stillness. These cherubic Nisei faces had fooled many a new teacher at Two Sloughs Elementary. Shiz's two sons were double trouble, for example. Tonight they had already managed to get hold of some "kachi kachi." They raced around the dance circle clacking their "kachi kachis" in the girls' faces, more or less in time to the drums. Ruth had learned to be careful about sending a note home to Japan Town about a poor test score or a disciplinary problem, though. Shame and dishonor were serious business in this community.

Shiz came by and urged Ruth to join the circle, but Ruth declined, content to listen to the music of the koto and the samisen, tapping the rhythm of the Taiko drum on her knee as the dancers moved forward, then back, turned, clapped…. She looked uncomfortably at Freddy Noble sitting beside her. "Sorry about that phone call this morning, Freddy," she muttered under her breath. "You've got to put the clamps on Lionel when it comes to guns."

"I know, Ruth. I know. Thanks for talking to him."

Which made Ruth feel even worse. She vowed to call the District Psychologist next week. She needed help with Lionel.

Now the men were dancing with their sons, sneakers and cuffed jeans poking out from under the boys' short *happi* kimonos as they followed their fathers' steps. A young army officer in uniform followed his father around the circle. Several teenagers in Bermuda shorts joined in behind him, watching Tosh. The Taiko drum beat more insistently. The pressure on these Nisei children was terrific. Three days a week they left Two Sloughs Elementary and went directly to Japanese School next to the Buddhist temple for Japanese language and arts lessons. That was where the children learned the dances. Ruth bargained with Mrs. Miyasaki, the Japanese teacher, for after-school time now and then when a band concert was coming up or she needed to do some math tutoring. Ruth and Mrs. Miyasaki had a sort of professional relationship that had helped Ruth a lot in dealing with the parents.

The youngest children grew bored with the dance and began to lark about in the center of the circle. The three little Sugimoto girls had been allowed to wear lipstick to match their red silk kimonos. They sat on the edge of the orchestra platform, their kimonos hiked up, applying lavish amounts of lipstick to one another. The youngest Ogawa twirled around the platform in what looked like a hand-me-down princess costume, obviously her favorite dress. Her hair was drawn back into a wispy ponytail, and she wore a bent crown. The smallest children had abandoned their shoes, running barefoot on the grass.

Doc Graham leaned across to Ruth, "We may have a problem developing over here. Tosh Nakamura was telling me before the dance that the Breams are raising the rents in Japan Town, nearly doubling them in a lot of cases."

"Bastards," Ruth whispered. She could feel Caroline Graham and Freddy Noble recoil in shock, but "bastards" was what she meant, and she was too angry to care who heard it. The Bream family owned most of the real estate and a good chunk of the farmland around the town of Two Sloughs. They were an odd, stingy, mean-spirited lot. Local legend had it that the patriarch of the family, old Thurgood Bream, Sr., a lawyer, had accumulated his wealth by writing wills for several Chinamen in town, then taking them out fishing in his row boat. When the Chinamen drowned in tragic fishing accidents, it was discovered that the deceased had left everything to old man Bream. This was only a fable, of course, but the story stuck because it rang so true to the present generation. "These houses in Japan Town are shacks, most of them," Ruth said. "The plumbing doesn't work half the time. These people pay too much rent as it is."

"You don't need to convince me." Doc Graham chuckled, "I make house calls."

"How can the Breams justify it? They haven't made a single improvement down here. Look at these roads -- just dirt, all rutted, no sidewalks. In winter they're impassable."

"They don't need to justify it, Ruth. They own the place."

"Does this have anything to do with that grandson they lost in the Coral Sea?" Ruth asked.

Doc shrugged. "Hard to guess. That kid was the apple of his grandfather's eye."

"Well, we'll have to come up with something," Ruth said. "We can't let them get away with this. I don't know why these families aren't more resentful as it is."

A warm breeze kicked up. The air felt soft against Ruth's face, as if she could rest her head on it. Crickets sang in the weeds. Frogs croaked in the back slough. A fat, orange moon, streaked with smoke from burning stubble, floated up over the horizon and slowly began to rise in the eastern sky, filling itself with the hot August night. Mrs. Nagoshi arrived with a platter of those delicious molded rice balls. "O-nigiri" she called them, and Ruth struggled to pronounce it. "They're so delicious. O-ni-gi-ri," she said with her mouth full. And yellow, pickled radish. Shiz had told her that Mrs. Nagoshi was jealous of her onigiri recipe and refused to share it. When pressed, she calmly copied out a recipe for, "very good onigiri."

"But," said Shiz, "it wasn't <u>her</u> onigiri."

Ruth took one more rice ball, bit into it, trying to figure out what was inside. Tosh and some of the other men passed out bottles of soft drinks and straws to the children.

"Know anybody in the health department?" Ruth asked Doc after Mrs. Nagoshi had moved away.

"What're you getting at?"

"Anybody who could get this whole neighborhood condemned for unsanitary conditions, unsafe electrical wiring or something?"

Doc Graham smiled, "Or who could threaten it if the rents went up?"

"Exactly," Ruth said.

"Ruth," Freddy Noble said in admiration, "you've got a real genius for warfare. You should've been a general."

Then how come I can't conquer your darned son, Lionel? thought Ruth, but the women had started to dance again. Some of the grandmothers had joined in, Mrs. Ogawa, Mrs. Matsubara in their house dresses, remembering the dances by heart. The children swirled around the center, all barefoot now, their obis and head sashes slipping, orange soda down the front of one little jacket. Obon celebrated a good son, a disciple of Buddha, who rescued his mother from some sort of hell. Ruth turned to enjoy the fragile beauty of the Obon dancers and the final prayer.

September

Ruth loved the first day of school at Two Sloughs Elementary. She couldn't help herself. Part of it was contagion. The children were excited, too, although they would have been hung by their thumbs with jump ropes before they would have admitted it. It was always too hot, and there was the usual confusion about where to put the migrant kids and the new batch of Chinese "cousins" that the Leong family produced every year, fresh from China. Ruth had developed a system on the Chinese children, who were generally boys about 12 to 14. She started them in kindergarten, and when they had mastered kindergarten English, she moved them up to first grade, and so on. They generally made it to the fourth or fifth grade by the end of the first year. Not an ideal arrangement, but the District Superintendent had told her not to take them at all. "We have no provisions for non-English speaking children," he said. "They probably aren't even legal." The District Superintendent gave her a pain in the neck. He had written her three or four serious letters "to share his concern" for her use of the word <u>kids</u> instead of <u>children</u>. "We must set an example," he wrote. "The term <u>kids</u> applies to the offspring of goats," he explained. "We must treat our young students with respect so that they in turn will show respect to us." Any man who had time to use the word <u>children</u> probably wasn't teaching enough of them. And as for respect, if anybody in the District commanded more respect from her students, Ruth would like to meet him. This toad was quick enough to "share his concern," but he was darned slow sharing textbooks and art materials and money, which she needed, and she needed now. She and the second grade teacher had spent a whole afternoon last week trying to scotch tape enough readers together to start school.

Still, as she stood in the hall at the beginning of the first recess, she couldn't help feeling as frisky as the youngsters. The boys all had that funny white line around their skulls from their first hair cuts since the beginning of summer. In their new striped T-shirts she thought they looked like freshly tonsured monks from some pygmy religious order. The girls wore new plaid dresses from Montgomery Ward with white collars and sashes that would pull out before the end of lunch recess. Even the migrant kids looked presentable. They were wearing clean T-shirts and shoes that fit fairly well, considering. She had told their mothers to cut the boys' hair or Ruth would do it herself, and the mothers had done a fair job of it. Only one class was seriously overcrowded. All in all, she was feeling pretty satisfied with herself.

So when Miss Malberger came puffing up the corridor toward her, Ruth's heart sank. Miss Malberger looked like a ball of fuzzy gray yarn that had been unraveled by malicious kittens. She wore her hair in a snarled bun at the back of her neck, but by first recess only the most loyal strands remained tucked in. Now the rest of her hair had escaped in frantic wisps about her head, her round face was red and fiercely swollen, and her glasses had slipped toward the end of her small nose. She clutched a manila envelope in her fat fist.

"Your office," Miss Malberger panted, and when they had closed the door, she sank into the chair in front of Ruth's desk and shoved the envelope across to Ruth.

Ruth knew that Marian Malberger was a top-notch teacher. She might look a little disheveled, but when it came to teaching a kid to read, this woman knew her business. It had been whispered around town that she took a drink or two at night, and that might be. Ruth didn't frankly see how a first grade teacher could survive <u>without</u> a drink or two at night. It unnerved Ruth to see the normally unflappable Miss Malberger so upset. It also relieved her to know that Lionel Noble wasn't in Miss Malberger's class. She opened the manila envelope.

"Whew," Ruth whistled after a minute or two. "I didn't know Chinese women were so athletic." She flipped slowly through the pictures. "In fact I'm not convinced it's physically possible to assume some of these positions, even with the aid of a garter belt." She peered more closely at the last picture. "Holy Mackerel!" She dropped the pictures on her desk and leaned back in her wood swivel chair. "Marian, I had no idea the first grade was so educational."

Marian started to laugh softly. She sagged in her chair, and she let her arms flop at her sides. Her broad blouse jiggled slightly and her short, fat legs sprawled out in front of her. "I learned a thing or two, I can tell you."

The two women sat staring at the Manila envelope.

"Now," said Marian, "the question is what are we two old maids going to do about it?"

Ruth sat up. She wasn't <u>that</u> old. Marian Malberger, great mound of ground round, could speak for herself. "Miss Hamburger," the children called her.

But, of course, Marian was right. They had to do something about the pictures. And recess was nearly over. "Harold Yee?" Ruth asked.

"Probably," Marian said. "His little brother Roland just started first grade. I imagine Harold accidentally slipped them in the wrong binder."

"Well, I'd better go see old man Yee, or the sixth grade will get more education than they bargained for."

"He won't be up this early," Marian warned.

"Then, he'll have to get up," Ruth said. "I'll tell Mr. Mundorf to hold down the fort until I get back." She grabbed her car keys and her handbag.

The Chinese settlement would have seemed picturesque to Ruth if she hadn't been so scared of rats. It was a silly fear that she admitted to no one, but the one thing she was skittish about was rats. She hoped Lionel Noble never found out. China Camp, as the locals called it, looked like an Old West town that had been hauled off the back lot of a Hollywood studio and dumped up-river from Two Sloughs. Worn wood store fronts faced the river -- vestiges of black paint spelled out the Yuen Chong Market. A wooden arch studded with burnt out light bulbs suggested the majestic remnants of the Star Theatre. Most of the stores along the boardwalk had been abandoned long ago. Ruth turned down off the levee, behind these store fronts, where a couple of dozen swaybacked two story buildings leaned out toward her on both sides of a narrow dirt alleyway. A tiny, hunched old woman shuffled in her cotton slippers along the uneven wood sidewalk, ignoring Ruth. Two old men sat on a splintered bench on the sunny side of the alley watching her.

Ruth parked her car in front of Al the Wop's, the one restaurant still in operation. It was closed, of course, so early in the morning. Only the grocery store and the mission church looked open. She headed for the boarded up store front two doors beyond Al's place. The Chinese characters over the doorway might have announced its purpose, but she doubted it. They were probably relics of some long-departed herb shop or hop house. Ruth banged on the door, waited a moment, then banged again. "Mr. Yee," she bellowed. "Mr. Yee, I need to talk." She banged again, louder.

A slender, young woman in a silk wrapper leaned out one of the upstairs windows. "Mr. Yee not at home," she said.

"You tell Mr. Yee to come talk, or I'll put his sons in jail," Ruth said.

The young woman ducked inside, a flash of turquoise silk, and a long silence followed.

Ruth looked up at the rusting corrugated roofs, the unpainted, silvery siding. Narrow balconies balanced high above the alley on thin, knock-kneed posts. Their rickety second story railings seemed strung together with clothesline and electric wire. A bare light bulb dangled by a single strand on the balcony above her. The windows were blind.

Presently a young man appeared at the window. "Uncle very sick. You come back later."

Ruth didn't know this young man. Not local, Ruth guessed. His clothes were too flashy. "You tell your uncle if he isn't down here in ten minutes, I'll call the sheriff and have both his sons put in jail, both Harold and Roland. You take him this." She slipped half the photographs out of the envelope and sailed the envelope with the remaining pictures up onto the balcony. "You tell him ten minutes." She waved the rest of the pictures. "I'll keep these," she said.

Across the street, a row of Crisco tins planted full of orange marigolds lined the upstairs railing. A skinny black cat peered down at Ruth between the broken rails. There were still two or three gambling houses and a "hop den" in operation, but Ruth couldn't begin to guess which abandoned-looking buildings still thrived.

Mr. Yee opened the door moments later. He bowed to Miss Hardy and stepped back courteously. A slender, elegant man, he wore a western suit and tie. He had a high forehead, sad, unblinking eyes that turned downward at the corners and a thin mustache that always reminded Ruth of the catfish she and her sister used to fish for in the river. Before the war, Mr. Yee had played saxophone in the Chinese Methodist Home Missionary Marching Band. He was one of the staunchest supporters of Ruth's school music program.

"You come, drink tea, please."

Ruth stood her ground, "Mr. Yee, you keep your two boys out of this whorehouse, or I'll tell the State, and they'll take them away from you. You understand me? No place for young boys. They're good boys, smart. No more dirty pictures in my school."

"I not know..."

"You be more careful. Especially with Harold. He's eleven. Eleven-year-old boys have big eyes. No joke, Mr. Yee." Ruth had the feeling that there were dozens of ears listening to her, although only the two old men were visible on the street. So much the better. At least a dozen of her students came from China Camp. Somebody would understand the full import of her words.

"Mr. Yee," she said quietly, "you've been a good father to those boys. Harold's homework is always perfect. The teachers have always remarked on Harold's homework. He scored in the top three per cent in the state math tests last year. He's headed for the university. Don't let him miss his chance."

"Miss Hardy, thank you. Thank you. Thank you. It hard here."

"I know it's hard, but you've got to keep them out of trouble."

"I talk to Harold."

Ruth looked at the father's worried face, "Good," she said. "I'll keep an eye on him, too." She thrust the rest of the pictures into Mr. Yee's arms. "No more dirty pictures in my school." She inclined her head. Mr. Yee bowed still deeper.

Ruth turned toward her car and saw the skinny black cat slip off the hood of her car and down a narrow alleyway. The alley had been swept with a twig broom so that the cat's paws made a track in the smooth, sunlit dust. Rusted Coca-Cola signs were nailed on the wall along the alley.

Driving back to school, she wrestled with the Yee family's situation. Mr. Yee ran the best brothel in the county. Everybody said so. Even the sheriff. She had had several of the girls' children in school, and the mothers had been conscientious about attendance, punctuality, homework. If Ruth ever ran into trouble, one word to Mr. Yee took care of it. Mr. Yee had told Ruth that he was saving for the boy's education. "University Money," he called it. She imagined there were fathers in town who were making money on more suspicious enterprises than Mr. Yee's and spending it in worse ways.

Fifteen minutes later she was back in her office, trembling slightly from the exertion and the horrifying images of those photographs. The phone rang.

"Oh, Freddy," she said. "No, I'm all right," she said. "Just a little excitement here.... No, not Lionel." Ruth laughed. "Not Lionel at all. What's on your mind?"

"Doc Graham came up with some old DPT vaccine. He ran into somebody from the county at a medical meeting. I've gone over all the papers. It should be fine, but we ought to use it before the end of the month, to be on the safe side. Could you set inoculations for next Thursday afternoon? Doc says he'll swing by around 2:00. You'll need release forms."

"Oh, Fred, you really are a brick," Ruth said, and then felt embarrassed to catch herself gushing. That had been one of her father's expressions, "You're a brick, Ruthie." He always called her Ruthie, her warm, easy-going father.

"You sure you're O.K., Ruth? You sound kinda' shaky. Why don't you come over at lunch time? I'll fix you up with a chocolate soda with coffee ice cream."

"Not on your life," snapped Ruth. "If I don't lay down the law in that lunchroom the first day of school, there'll be peanut butter from hell to breakfast."

Freddy was daunted. "So long then," he said and hung up.

Ruth sat at her desk with the receiver still in her hand. She shouldn't have been so brusque. It was only because sitting at the Two Sloughs Pharmacy and Soda Fountain with Freddy, sipping a chocolate soda made with coffee ice cream sounded so lovely, so appealing. Oh, darn, now she was two minutes late ringing the lunch bell.

Ruth and Doc Graham went way back. Between the two of them, they knew nearly every ugly secret the town harbored. They had entered into innumerable pacts with the various Devils of Two Sloughs in exchange for the souls of the town's children. They had dealt with incest and roughed up wives and beaten kids and bastard babies. Neither of them had actually ever broken the law. They just followed the law on a kind of a long tether, depending on the circumstances, the family, the children's welfare.

But Ruth didn't know everything. That evening Ruth dropped by the Grahams' house on her way home from school, about 5:30. She wanted to tell Doc she had set up the immunization program, and, to tell the truth, she hoped Caroline Graham would insist she stay for a drink. Southern hospitality and all. Doc mixed the best Old Fashioneds in town, methodically, as if he were in a medical lab, the bitters, the sugar cube, the orange peel. And the conversation at the Grahams was always good. Caroline subscribed to The Saturday Review and The New Yorker, and Doc had one of those rangy, restless minds that roves from astronomy to Renaissance art to Bach. Last year he had become obsessed with Leonardo da Vinci. He'd sent away for an immense book of Leonardo's drawings and notes. Caroline saved articles for Ruth, a review of a new recording by Jussi Boerling, a piece on seed catalogs from The New Yorker. After a long day of chicken pox and chewing gum, Ruth found the Graham's living room an oasis.

She raised her fist to knock on the kitchen screen door -- nobody in Two Sloughs ever went to the front door -- just as Doc opened the door and looked dazedly out at her through the screen. Behind him, Caroline Graham's voice shrieked, "You're a goddamn liar, and you know it. You're cheating on me. You dump me in this stinking backwater when you could've done orthopedics in Sacramento. You dump me here, and then you go off tomcattin'." Caroline Graham, first soprano in the church choir, the only woman in town whose stocking seams were always straight, whose gloves were always white, Caroline Graham, who claimed to come from a very good family in Charleston, South Carolina -- and had the solid silver punch bowl to prove it -- Caroline Graham rushed into the kitchen after him, stark naked, livid with anger, wielding a golf club. A putter. Her small, perfect mouth was distorted with rage. She gripped the putter with both hands, squared her naked hips around and slammed the putter against a kitchen counter, so absorbed in her fury that she was oblivious to Ruth outside the screen door. She turned her back and disappeared into the dining room, but Ruth could still hear her:

"I can't imagine what woman would have you anyway. You're no kind of a lover. You don't know the least thing about satisfying a woman. You don't have an ounce of romance in that puny cock. You can never even...."

Doc and Ruth stared at each other helplessly through the screen door.

"I've come at a bad time," Ruth said, backing away from the door. "I should've called."

Doc reached behind him and closed the door softly. "I'll walk you out to your car." They walked silently to the street, and Ruth got into her car. She leaned out the open window. Doc patted her arm. "Marriage can be kind of a mine field," he said.

On the river road, headed out of town, Ruth cut the bad curve too wide. She swerved back over to her side of the road. Dear God, she thought, I'm driving too fast. Caroline Graham, the town's top candidate for the Good Housekeeping Seal of Approval. Dear God. She hurried past a gang of boys digging in the levee. She should have stopped to investigate. The kids dug secret pits and caves into the river levees, which were mostly made of sand. They camouflaged the entrances with willow because their fathers destroyed the caves any time they found them. They were too dangerous. They weakened the levees. The sandy soil collapsed too easily. (Doc tomcatting? With whom?) Ricky Scoleri had been caught in a cave-in. They'd had to dig out his leg. But the sand levees also gave way easily to the boys' shovels, and they built caves and pits roofed with rotting planks that held three or four kids crowded in a circle. Ruth and her sister Jeanie had dug the same pits a generation before. They had lit candle stubs and stuck them in tuna fish cans in sandy niches in the damp walls, and they had smoked pipe weed. Billy Hawkins had stuck his finger up her underpants once in exactly such a cave. It was terrifying knowing the whole levee bank could come down on you at any minute, and it was secret and dark and forbidden. She should have stopped to investigate. She drove right by.

Ruth lived a mile out of town in an old foreman's cottage on the Giannini ranch. When she came to town as a young schoolteacher twelve years ago, the School Board arranged for her to rent this one story white frame house back behind the Giannini pear orchard. At first she was nervous out here, with nothing but cornfields and ditches all around her. Now she loved it. It had a front porch and a back garden. It was enough removed from the town of Two Sloughs so that she could come home at night, as she did now, change into her old khaki pants and her Keds, get a beer out of the refrigerator, put her Puccini on the record player full blast and stretch out on her redwood chaise in the backyard facing the Shasta daisies.

She couldn't shake the image of Doc comforting her at her car window. "Marriage can be kind of a mine field." Dear God. Doc comforting her! It dawned on her that Doc, who'd listened to everybody's troubles in town at one time or other, probably had no one to tell his troubles to. It had never occurred to Ruth before tonight that he even had troubles. Caroline Graham standing naked, skinny, rigid with fury, deriding Doc's "puny cock." Ruth closed her eyes and took a sip of her beer.

Caroline's voice had awakened memories of her mother's vindictive tone. Not the vocabulary, of course, or the Southern accent. Elizabeth Hardy's family came from Lowell, Massachusetts, and although it was several generations ago, the girls and their father were never allowed to forget it. Ruth recognized with a sinking sensation the similarity to Caroline Graham's roots in Charleston, South Carolina. Caroline and her mother even sang the same high, brittle soprano in the church choir. Different choirs, different women. But somehow the events of the day had become entangled. Caroline's obscenities, the dirty pictures at school, the China Camp whorehouse, Caroline's pointed breasts, the forbidden sand caves, the calendar at Ike's. Her mother's hypercritical soprano voice merged with Caroline's sarcastic southern drawl. Doc's battle-weary face faded into her father's sorry expression.

Marian Malberger's words came back to her, "What are we two old maids going to do about it?" Ruth leaned back and closed her eyes. "Il perche, non so," sang Puccini's Mimi, to the accompaniment of tree frogs. You can say that again, thought Ruth.

Ruth Hardy loved scrambled eggs on toast. She belonged to the cook-em-slow, cook-em-gentle school. Her father had been a great egg scrambler: a dollop of cream, a pinch of salt, nice and loose. Not watery, mind you, not runny. On his day off, her father would set a breakfast tray for her mother, which the girls would decorate with short stemmed geraniums stuffed in a cream pitcher. They would get down a fancy plate and cup from the top shelf. Their father would scramble the eggs while the girls made toast, scraping the burnt edges in the sink until everything looked just right. Then they'd appear at their mother's bedroom door singing "Good Morning to you. Good morning to you. We're all in our places..." in three part harmony. Every Sunday her mother would pretend to be surprised. She'd laugh delightedly, her hair down, her glasses off. She seemed so young on those Sunday mornings with her hair falling softly around her shoulders, so happy.

Now, during the week, Ruth fixed herself a bowl of corn flakes, but on Saturdays she took her time about breakfast, scrambled her eggs, did the crossword, helped herself to a second cup of coffee and another piece of toast with apricot jam. Every year Harvey Lemmon brought her a box of Royal Blenheim apricots, and she made jam from her mother's recipe.

Of course the whole meal hinged on the toast, so she was doubly pleased when Charlene Jepsen drove up to the front of her house on that first Saturday of school, even though she hadn't finished the crossword. She liked Charlene, and besides that Charlene Jepsen made the best cracked wheat bread in town. Charlene had a lot of talents. She was "artistic." In Two Sloughs they kept the labels short. Charlene was "artistic." Charlene's best friend Mavis was "pretty." Retta Mae Henderson was "good." Ruth was "brainy," which was the opposite of "pretty."

Charlene waved through the kitchen window, came in without knocking, put a loaf of bread on the table and sank down in one of the kitchen chairs, "She's started organizing her own funeral, for Christ's sake. I can't stand it. You got your hair cut. I like it. Frames your face."

It took Ruth a minute to untangle Charlene's snarled sentences. When Ruth read about "stream of consciousness" she always thought of Charlene. (Charlene's husband Larry put it more succinctly, "Every sentence out of that woman's mouth sounds as if she picked it up at a rummage sale. It doesn't go with anything else.") Ruth poured two cups of coffee and sat down across from Charlene.

"Oh, boy," Ruth said.

"Well Mavis always was a doer," said Charlene. She shook her head and smiled. "Your hair looks real pretty short. It kind of fluffs."

Charlene was one of those dark women whose face lit up when she smiled. She turned vivid, as if a spotlight had been turned on. She had dark hair, a big mouth and gypsy coloring. She pulled her thick hair back into a pony tail, tied with a brilliant scarf.

"And Mavis loves a good party, so it was probably natural, but three pages of instructions, real explicit, in that perfect penmanship of hers...."

Now Ruth knew as well as the next guy that a funeral can suffer from too much organization. Planning a funeral ought to be something like cooking with leftovers, a kind of desperation move after a series of big events -- a lot of loose ends and everybody frazzled. You couldn't do it again, but it's right for the moment. You start getting out cookbooks and following recipes, and you end up with peas in library paste or worse. A funeral is like that.

"Oh boy," she said again.

"It's awful. I can't hardly stand to go over there any more. She's worked it all out with Retta Mae, every last detail. Retta Mae isn't even her best friend."

Retta Mae was sort of the plump, Presbyterian patron saint of Two Sloughs. She was wacky enough to put you off balance and bossy enough in that "Now-Ruth-honey-everybody-loves-those-chicken-sandwiches-of-yours--You-make-the-chicken-sandwiches" kind of way. It seemed that Ruth's cakes were too lopsided for some people's taste, and her pie crust was unpredictable. But not much had happened in Two Sloughs without one of her chicken sandwiches alongside it. Only floods. For floods she made chicken soup with barley. And Retta Mae generally took charge. Retta Mae saved stray cats, unwed mothers and meadowlarks with bent wings. She collected money for refugee relief, canned goods for Christmas baskets and popsicle sticks. (Ruth couldn't remember why she collected popsicle sticks.) If there was a problem in town, Retta Mae would be in it right up to her chicken wattle chin.

But Charlene was Mavis's best friend, had been since high school. They'd marched side by side on the Elk Grove High School marching drill team. "Green and purple, green and purple...." They still launched into their routine at parties if they got enough bourbon in them. They'd gone together to the Grand Assembly of the Order of Rainbow Girls in Santa Cruz, where they ate great gobs of cotton candy at the Boardwalk and threw up on the Rip Tide Ride. They'd been bridesmaids in each other's weddings.

"Charlene, I'm sorry. Maybe Mavis is trying to protect you. And you know Retta Mae. She's just trying to be helpful. Charlene's eyes blazed, "Why is it that woman always makes me want to respond with a four letter word?"

Ruth laughed. "Too much goodness. Steady diet of it can give you indigestion."

Charlene put her elbows on the table and rubbed her temples, "I'm not behaving well. I know that. I just want to sit around Mavis's dinette table and drink coffee and eat powdered sugar doughnuts like we used to. But she's so wrapped up in this dying business. She keeps wanting to talk about it, and I can't stand it. It's like watching previews of coming attractions of movies you don't want to see."

"You've been a good friend to Mavis, Charlene. For a lot of years. That counts for something."

" I guess. You know what? I kind of dwell on my failures. I can skip right over my successes, but I dwell on my failures. Weird, huh?"

"Oh, I don't know. We all do a lot of 'what if-ing.' My mother was the grand champion 'If only I hadn't...'"

"Yeah," said Charlene, "Do you ever wonder if..." She hesitated, changed her mind, changed it again, "...if you should have gotten married when the rest of us did, had a life of your own?"

"I've got a life of my own," Ruth said carefully. "I don't get much time to live it. That's all."

"I mean a life with men in it," Charlene said. "Oh, hell, not that.... not that men are any great shakes, come to think of it. One great big ego rubbed raw. I just wish... I don't know...."

"You sure this isn't a case of misery loves company, Charlene?"

Charlene hooted, "Could be. Could be."

Charlene popped her clutch, lurched off, raising dust on the road. Old Man Giannini would give her hell if he saw her, she thought, raising dust like that. She shouldn't be telling anybody how to lead her life, she thought, least of all Ruth. Charlene roared past the DEAD SLOW sign that old man Giannini had painted. Charlene's life ran late and on empty. A chaotic, disorderly life, a kitchen drawer kind of life, full of clutter. She entertained her friends, but they knew better than to rely on her. She frustrated her children. She confused her husband. ("You're always blind-siding me," he complained once. "I never know where you're gonna come from next.") She had always had a poor sense of direction, and she sometimes felt herself spinning crazily in circles, weaving unsteadily, dizzy from her passage through life, tripped up by surprising obstacles she herself had left in the way. She was a great one to give advice.

Ruth watched Charlene drive off raising dust. Ruth wondered what Charlene had really wanted to ask her. What was really eating Charlene? Charlene wore the fidgety, flat-eared look of a horse about to kick. Why was she feeling so rebellious?

Charlene had spoken of marriage in the past tense for Ruth. "Do you ever wonder if you should have gotten married?" she'd asked. Was Ruth too old to get married all of a sudden? Was there a season, like duck hunting? Then it's over? Ruth was supposed to be the "brainy" one. She ought to be able to come up with more answers.

It wasn't the staying after school for a whole week that bothered Jimmy Martin. He and Miss Hardy got along O.K. Miss Hardy talked straight and seriously to Jimmy, and Jimmy was a straight and serious kind of kid, a skinny kid, with a stammer and a cowlick and enormous feet that flopped ahead of him when he walked down the hall.

Harold Yee had to stay after school the whole first week, too, because of some dirty pictures nobody even got to see. Miss Hardy had found them too quick. Harold invited Jimmy home for main meal one afternoon during their week of "after school." Harold and his little brother Roland lived in China Camp with their aunt and uncle, in rooms back of the Yuen Chong market. The two boys walked home together along the railroad tracks, catching grasshoppers as they went. Harold's uncle was working behind the butcher counter slicing steaks when the boys walked in. He offered the boys each a raw hot dog, which they smoked like cigars for a while and then ate. Harold's aunt stood at the cash register. Sometimes she let them take bubble gum right out of the glass counter without paying, so they loitered around hoping for a hand out, but she was adding up figures on her abacus, and she was in a bad mood.

"Cummon," said Harold, and he and Jimmy followed old Grandfather as he scuffed like a straggly old crow along the dark back hall to feed his snails. He caught the snails in the sloughs and kept them in a dishpan on the back porch. The snails struggled to smooch their way up the sides of the dishpan, but the slick enamel surface defeated them. They kept falling backwards to the bottom of the pan. The boys watched them struggle, watched them ooze, watched them defecate, watched them crawl over one another. (They're fucking, Harold promised.) They tortured the occasional snail that managed to work his slimy way to the top of the dishpan, flicking him back into the water.

"Good to eat," said Grandfather. He had about six teeth in his mouth, randomly spaced, studded with gold, so they flashed when he talked. "Real good. You try. In restaurant you pay big bucks," he said picking out the biggest snail, holding it up to Jimmy's face.

Grandmother sat, small and shrunken as a dried mushroom, at the oilcloth-covered table in the kitchen, criticizing Harold's aunt's preparation of main meal. As Jimmy sat on a dinette chair watching Harold's aunt sizzle things in a big wok on the stove, Grandmother aimed her sharp tongue at Jimmy.

"What's she saying? What's she mad about?" he asked Harold.

Harold giggled. "She says, 'Chinese marry White, make ugly babies.' She smokes. It makes her crazy sometimes."

Harold said they didn't eat the snails. "They're my Grandfather's pets," he said. "Grandfather's crazy, too." And Jimmy didn't actually see anybody eat a snail at Harold's house. It was mostly soup with slippery noodles and long green strings floating in it. Jimmy poked around his soup pretty carefully with his chopstick. He didn't see anything that looked like a snail, dead or alive. He heaped his bowl with sticky rice, which he loved, and which didn't have anything weird in it.

Of course, Jimmy had complained mightily at the dinner table at his house the night of the BB gun episode that it wasn't fair, that <u>he</u> hadn't done anything. But he got no sympathy from his mother and father.

"If you're going to play with Lionel Noble, you'd better get used to trouble, because that's what that boy is," said his mother. Even his sister Sally, who was a year older and turning into a real simp, in Jimmy's opinion, boy crazy and horse crazy all at the same time, was no help. Sally hated Lionel. Because of the Fourth of July Parade. What bothered Jimmy about staying after school was that it was September, and he was parted from his beloved boat. He had secretly named his boat "The Avenger," but he didn't tell anybody. He just called it "the boat" in an off-hand kind of way. He'd picked pears for his Dad all summer, piecework, to earn enough money for it. Up at 4:30, before daylight, when the orchards were still wet and cold, picking up "grounders," fallen fruit, in the scratchy weeds beneath the trees, dragging full buckets of pears, half-asleep, hungry, arms already aching. At sunrise, when the sun lit the treetops and the birds sat in the topmost branches and dragonflies and moths flitted through the tall grass, he stopped to eat the corn muffins his mom had put in his jacket pocket the night before. Then for a minute the orchard looked beautiful. The shivering pickers, in their threadbare shirts, began to warm up. They sang and laughed in the trees.

But then the heat turned heavy, and by midday Jimmy could hardly breathe. The pickers yelled at him when he got in their way as they ran to move their three-legged ladders from tree to tree. They teased him in Spanish, giving him nicknames he couldn't understand. Only Digal, the thin, bent-over Filipino who had worked for his grandfather, took pity on him. At the end of every row, Jimmy would find an extra bucket or two of pears that Digal had left for him.

Finally, three weeks before school started, he and his Dad drove down to Rio Vista with the proceeds of his summer in cash, $78.35, on the seat between them. Jimmy purchased a used eight foot wooden boat with a planked front deck, bench seats, removable oar locks, four smelly but serviceable orange life jackets, and a one and a half horsepower Evinrude outboard motor with gas can. She was a beaut.

"Hardly a pimple on her," his Dad said.

After they loaded it into the back of his Dad's pickup, Mr. Sherman at the Marina threw in a set of oars and a rope. "That'd be your bow line, Son," Mr. Sherman said. "Now that you own a boat, you ought to know the lingo."

When they got home, Dan Martin drew a diagram for Jimmy that showed bow and stern, port and starboard. Jimmy spent a whole day on the front lawn with a brush and a hose, scrubbing the little boat until it shone. He wiped the engine down with a rag dipped in gasoline, the way his father had taught him. He painstakingly painted the wood rail around the top of the boat bright orange ("flame orange" the paint can said,) but he didn't paint a name on the boat. He didn't even tell Lionel. Only he knew it was "The Avenger." He and his Dad carried it over the levee that evening and tied it up under the big cottonwood on the river in front of their house.

He'd never known such sweet independence. Every morning he and Lionel would make a pile of peanut butter and jelly sandwiches, fill a quart jar of water and take off. Jimmy was a cautious kid, but he yearned for adventure. The thing about Lionel was that exciting things happened when Lionel was along. Jimmy loved that. They headed for the sloughs behind China Camp, which were twisted and confusing and choked with tules and lily pads. Both boys were scared of getting lost in the thousand murky back sloughs that never looked the same twice, or kidnapped by the old Chinamen who lurked along the banks fishing. They were afraid of the beaver who had ferocious teeth, and the water snakes who lifted their heads out of the water and eyed them with yellow eyes, and the hawks who swooped down on them if they came close to a nest. The banks of the deserted back islands bristled with stinging nettles and blackberry thorns, and the wild grapevines drooped ominously from the overhanging trees. They thought the sucking mud along the banks was probably quick sand. All in all, it was a perfect place for two eleven-year-old boys.

Their fathers discussed the situation one morning at Ike's. "Think they're safe out there?" Lionel's father, Freddy, had asked.

"Well, safe as eleven year old boys ever are," Dan Martin said.

"They're good swimmers," Fred said.

"What do you think, Bud?"

Bud Zolinsky was an old Russian fur trapper who had drifted down from the Alaskan gold fields about the turn of the century. He lived on a houseboat out back of China Camp and still trapped beaver and mink out there, some of it legal; some not. He supplied the Chinese with frogs and turtles and the Black Bass that was their favorite fish. He kept bees. He wore his hat with the earflaps and his irrigating boots summer and winter. You wanted a fresh salmon or a jar of honey, he was the guy to talk to. He never said much at Ike's, but he was the local authority on the back sloughs.

"Hell," Bud shrugged, "this time of year.... Tell 'em always to set off upstream. That way, they get into trouble, they float back down."

Staying after school meant an end to their boating for one whole week in September, which is the best month on the sloughs. The afternoons are still warm, the grapes and blackberries are ripe, and the water is slow and green. The Saturday after their one-week banishment from the river, they decided upon an all-day excursion. Janet Martin was nervous about it. Dan Martin, on appeal, said they could go. "Use your heads, is all, and take the oars. I don't ever want you out there without oars and lifejackets."

They fortified their rations with a quart of Kool-Aid and a package of Hydrox cookies. They were planning a trip to the Meadows, a wide marsh that verged on Georgeanna Slough, wound with the myriad waterways behind China Camp. Their plan was to make a map as they went along so that they could find their way back.

They putted off and got to the slough behind China Camp without too much trouble. Lionel's map looked pretty good.

"I could sure use one of them Chinese cucumbers right now," Lionel said. "Maybe we could sneak over the levee and steal one."

"We don't have time," Jimmy said nervously. "We still got a long way."

"They've got jillions of 'em this time of year. They wouldn't care a bit," Lionel said.

"I'm not crazy about cucumbers," Jimmy lied. "They make you fart."

"Chicken," Lionel said. "Fraid of those old Chinamen."

"Am not."

"Are too."

Jimmy had spent more time in China Camp than Lionel had. Jimmy knew strange things went on in China Camp. Old people with hidden eyes and clacking tongues ate weird, slimy things and got mad at white boys.

"I am not chicken. I don't want to take the time," Jimmy said.

"Chicken," muttered Lionel under his breath. "Plock-plock- plock-plock..."

So they eased into the bank behind China Camp, tied the boat, and snuck up over the levee into the Chinese vegetable gardens behind the town. Peering through the dried mustard stalks, they could see a dozen little twig-fenced plots, jungles of thick vines and muddy rows of fat green plants. A couple of old men hoed in their plots, but the garden nearest them looked empty. A fence of lashed willow, all bound and woven, encircled the plot. Along the far side, long beans hung from bamboo trellises. Cabbages big as a man's head stood in a row beside them and then rows of onions and leafy things. They were lucky. On the near side of the garden shed that stood in the middle of the plot were the bumpy, green bitter melons and the long cucumbers.

"We'll slip in past the shed and grab a cucumber and be out of there," Lionel whispered.

"What if somebody's in the shed?"

"There isn't room. Look. It's just for tools."

The shed was small, sided with old lumber, roofed with a rusty Mobil Oil sign. Old coffee cans in front of the shack held seedlings.

The two boys crept into the plot, crouching low. Lionel snatched a cucumber, and they turned back toward the shack without a sound. Between them and the wire gate stood an ancient man shaking a hoe.

"Uh oh," Lionel said and sprinted toward the willow fence.

Jimmy followed him and managed to wriggle between the poles just before the old man's hoe came down behind him. The old man yelled horrible things at them in Chinese. Now all the old men were probably chasing them. They probably had knives. The two boys raced over the levee, and at the top Jimmy's huge foot caught a root. He fell flat. Lionel looked around and stopped, ran back,

"Quick, Jimmy, get up." Lionel pulled Jimmy up, then heaved the cucumber as far as he could back down the levee toward the Chinaman. They scrambled into the rowboat. Lionel pushed off, grabbed the oars. "Get that thing going," puffed Lionel as he pulled on the oars, but Jimmy was already yanking the starter rope of his outboard motor. "Row, damn it," Jimmy shot back, and Lionel was rowing, but in his haste he kept skipping along the top of the water with his oars. He was doing more splashing than rowing. "Watch it!" Jimmy said, "Watch what you're doing."

Finally the motor caught, and they got around the bend, out of sight. But Lionel didn't stop rowing, and Jimmy kept the motor revved.

"You and your stupid cucumbers," Jimmy shouted above the noise of the motor.

"You and your big feet," Lionel shouted back. "We would've been outta there, no problem."

"Oh yeah? What about the guy in the shed?"

And all the while Lionel rowed and Jimmy kept the one and a half horsepower motor at full throttle. They turned further and further back into the sloughs until it looked completely wild to them, and they thought they might be safe.

Lionel put the oars down. "I bet they would have killed us," he gasped.

Jimmy idled the motor, "If they hadn't, my Dad would've," Jimmy said.

"Not mine," said Lionel.

"Go on," said Jimmy crossly.

"No, it's true. He would've just said how he was 'disappointed.' Seems like he don't care about anything any more."

"Well, don't worry," said Jimmy. "My Dad would've killed us both."

"So where's the map?" Jimmy asked, and the boys looked down into the bottom of the boat at the map, floating in two inches of water. It didn't matter. They'd lost the pencil, and they hadn't taken notes during their escape anyway. They were lost.

From then on the adventure seemed doomed. They'd gotten turned around some way in their escape, and instead of widening out into the Meadows, the sloughs got narrower, murkier. The banks were crisscrossed with otter runs. They smelled of mud and widgeon grass and dead fish. The current seemed to be flowing the wrong way. All the islands looked the same and unfamiliar. They watched for a place where they might scramble up a levee and get their bearings, but they were too far back in the sloughs. Nobody lived here. There were no levees. These islands were just floating peat bogs, clumps of cattails and water lilies and duckweed swimming in the mud. They even cut the motor and listened for the sound of a tractor or a truck, but the sloughs were silent in the heat of the afternoon. They'd lost the cucumber, so they ate the cookies and then the sandwiches.

Around every bend they hoped for a tree or a bridge or a barn, some landmark they remembered. At every fork in the twisting channel they argued over which way to go. Now there appeared to be no current at all. The shadows lengthened, and the end-of-the-season monster mosquitoes came out, buzzing around their ears, biting the backs of their knees and between their toes.

"I promised Dad we'd be home by sundown," Jimmy said.

"Swell," said Lionel

Jimmy shook the gas can. "We're low on gas."

Something made a big splash in the slough right behind them. They both turned to see a huge ring of concentric ripples welling up where whatever it was had gone under.

Jimmy cut the motor, "What was that?"

Lionel pulled the oars into the boat, "Too big for a muskrat."

They sat motionless, listening, looking into the murky water all around them.

"Sometimes people let those baby pet alligators go," said Lionel. "They end up out in swamps. Huge. I read that."

"Where?" demanded Jimmy.

"I dunno."

They sat swatting mosquitoes, listening.

"Man, I'd hate to die out here." Lionel said.

"Cripes! We're not going to die. We're a little lost is all."

"But we could die, of starvation, thirst. My mom did."

"Baloney. Your mom died of a car accident."

"Well, she died."

Lionel sat hunched in the front of the rowboat with his hands over his ears because of the mosquitoes.

"Look, Lionel, I'm taking every right fork in the slough. If that doesn't work, we'll try left forks. Now row while we have some light left."

But it was the dusk that saved them.   As their motor began to sputter and their stomachs began to rumble with hunger, they saw the lanterns of the fisherman from China Camp far down the slough. By skirting them quietly, they were able to get home just as the light of the sunset left the river, changing it from gold to a brassy black.

Sally stood on the bank watching for them anxiously. Once she made them out in the dark, she sang out, "Boy, are you in for it," and scooted over the levee to tell her parents.

"Do you think the Chinaman told on us?" Lionel whispered.

"No, Dad's mad because Mom's worried."

Dan and Freddy both came down to the river's edge to meet the boys. "You're late," said Dan. "What happened?"

"We were headed to the Meadows, and we got lost."

"We got in a hurry, and we didn't keep track of left, right, you know, the turn-offs." Lionel said.

"You learn anything?" asked Dan.

"Yeah, not to be in such a darned hurry," Jimmy said, looking straight at Lionel.

Ruth kept her promise to herself and called the District Child Psychologist, a tall, round shouldered woman with big teeth, a great appreciation of baseball and the irritating habit of using the pronoun "we." The two women had become friends over the years. Both single, they met in Sacramento for the rare symphony or their mutual passion, The Sacramento Solons baseball team.

Ursula Brown came down from Sacramento to Two Sloughs Elementary after school on the following Wednesday. The two women sat in Ruth's office catching up on their vacations, gossip of the District Office, and latest reports on their baseball team.

"They've missed you," Ursula said. "Their pitching stinks, their ace short stop is out with a hamstring, and they can't get a hit to save themselves. They just aren't executing."

Ruth sighed. Her father had played catcher for the Rio Vista Rockets, the team sponsored by the local Chevrolet dealership. He'd played baseball with his girls by the hour in the backyard. One-a-cat, two-a-cat. They learned how to square around, keep the bat head low, and lay down a mean bunt. He taught them how to tag a runner, steal a base, hit to the off-field, head still, eye on the ball.

"I've got to get up there before the end of the season," she said. "I miss it." Ruth still kept score when she went to baseball games with Ursula, meticulously, with a fountain pen, the way her father had taught her.

"Call me. I'll get us tickets. So, we have a little trouble in the sixth grade, do we?" Ursula said, getting down to business.

"No, I have big trouble with one particular kid."

"Have we discussed him before?" asked Ursula.

"As a matter of fact, we have," said Ruth with a sigh. "Just about once a year for six years. Ursula, he's driving me crazy. I simply can't get through to him."

"Refresh my memory," said Ursula.

"He's the only child of a widower here in town, a really nice guy, sensitive, musical. The local Pharmacist. Went to Cal. Ahead of me, though. But he's just hopeless when it comes to discipline. I mean, he just flunks the course." Ursula cocked her head as if she'd heard a whistle.

"I've tried and tried to drum it into his head that he has to take this kid in hand," Ruth continued. "He can't seem to see that this kid is crying out for discipline."

There was a short pause. Ursula asked gently, "Ruth, are we talking about the son or about the father?"

Ruth colored slightly under Ursula's long gaze, "Well, that's all just background. I thought you people liked background. The problem is that I can't get through to this kid."

"Why do you think that is exactly?"

Occasionally Ursula drove Ruth crazy. Ruth wanted answers, not more questions. Ruth was a direct woman. She liked people who looked you in the eye and .... Actually, she couldn't fault Ursula for that. Ursula was looking at Ruth right now as if she were taking x-rays. Ruth half expected Ursula to say, "Now, hold your breath...." Ruth shifted uncomfortably.

"What's changed since we talked about him last?" Ursula asked.

"I think the kid hates me," she said.

"And that bothers you."

"Well, of course it bothers me, Ursula. I mean, how am I going to get anywhere with him if he hates me?"

"I see. And where exactly do you want to get with this boy?"

Ruth could see right through this line of inquiry, and it made her blood boil. Ursula had read too many romance novels over the summer. "Into the seventh grade is where I want to get with him," Ruth said tartly, "and then into the eighth grade, and then I want him the hell out of here."

Ursula sighed. "All right, Ruth, play it your way. But what's going on here?"

Ruth described the BB gun episode, and Ursula probed, asked more questions. But Ruth had the unsettling feeling that Ursula was more interested in Ruth than she was in Lionel. Exasperated, Ruth stopped mid-sentence, "<u>Lionel</u> is the problem, Ursula. I'm <u>fine</u>."

Ursula slumped back in her chair. "I have this unprofessional hunch that there's more going on here." She put her pen down. "Off the record, I'd say you've gotten yourself emotionally involved some way. I can't figure out whether it's with the son or the father. We're going to have to sort out your feelings before we can help the boy. We...."

"Of course I'm emotionally involved, Ursula. I'm frustrated as all hell!"

"Yes, but is it with the boy or his father?"

"Ursula, this is <u>me</u> you're talking to."

"I know, Ruth," Ursula said, "an attractive, single woman in a small town." She laughed at Ruth's horrified expression, "And the best second baseman in the District. I can give you all the advice in the world on getting through to the son." She reached down for her brief case and her purse, "Unfortunately, I don't know much about getting through to the father."

Ursula left Ruth feeling more confused than ever. Sometimes she wondered how the School District could spend thousands of dollars a year on psychology when what they needed was math books and ruled paper and mimeograph ink. She packed up and went home without even clearing her desk.

Mr. Mundorf couldn't believe it when he came in to her office with his duster. "Hope nothing was wrong with her," he thought, and then he remembered that there was never anything wrong with Miss Hardy.

When Ruth got home she changed into her baggy old khaki pants and her tennis shoes and went for a walk to let off some steam. She'd picked a good evening for it. She walked the dirt road along the edge of the cornfield behind her house -- just stubble now. The corn was all in. She headed straight out beside the field, walking briskly, away from the levee, out toward the middle of the island until the horizon lay perfectly circular around her, low and flat. She stood surrounded by an empty bowl of an autumn sky beginning to fill with the haze of burnt fields and Bay fog.

She was lonely. It came to her as she stood there smelling the burnt stubble and the dry weeds. She wanted somebody to talk to. She wanted to tell somebody that she'd grown up in the Delta, twenty miles downstream, and it seemed to her the only place where the sky was wide enough for sunsets. She wanted to say, "Look," to somebody as streaks of purple half a horizon long stretched out across the western rim. She wanted somebody to watch with her as the sun slipped out of its pale blue overturned bowl, down behind the flat earth. She saw splashes of gold and pink and finally crimson flow all around the rim. It was a good sky tonight, she wanted to say. The autumn skies were always best. Two sparrow hawks worked the field the way they did at sunset, starting on opposite ends and seeming to ignore each other. Suddenly they soared straight up to do a flighty minuet together in the open sky, a kind of dip and curtsy, and then off they flew in opposite directions, gilded by the last light. The sun was beginning to set earlier now. It was time for Ruth to go in, too.

She crossed a drainage ditch on an old plank and walked back along the neighboring field of corn stubble, a route she often took. The sky had faded. The skeletons of empty weeds along the ditch curled now; the dry corn stalks rattled hollow and brown. Even the orchard tucked up next to the levee seemed exhausted, as if the harvest had sapped all its energy. The leaves on the trees were dull. Branches broken by the weight of the fruit or by the careless placement of a ladder still hung akimbo. The land looked depleted once the sun went down, forlorn. She hadn't realized how tired she was. She picked up her pace. What she needed was a bowl of soup and a good night's sleep.

Ruth was on her way to the Post Office the next morning when the idea of a glazed doughnut and a cup of coffee stopped her dead in her tracks. It was good to drop by Ike's every once in a while when she didn't need anything, she rationalized, but she had her heart set on a glazed doughnut. Ike's was more raucous than usual this morning. Some argument was going on about who should buy coffee:

"So, the way I figure it, Scoleri ought to buy the whole town coffee, the damage he did, putting ideas in his little girl's head..." Bill Kramer was talking.

"No," Joe Scoleri said. "Martin owes us. Anybody who sets that ambulating glue factory loose in our town..."

Ruth was alarmed, "What happened?"

Ike poured her coffee. "Don't pay any attention to them, Ruth. They're still rehashing the Fourth of July Parade. Glazed?"

"Thanks, Ike. How <u>was</u> the parade this year? Did I miss anything?"

Every head in Ike's turned to Ruth.

"You mean you haven't heard?" Ike asked.

"Unhuh," said Ruth, her mouth full of glazed doughnut.

"Well it all started when Scoleri took his daughter Susie down to the Grand National Rodeo at the Cow Palace in San Francisco," said Bill Kramer. "Of all the damn fool ideas."

"Hey," said Joe Scoleri, "Travel broadens a little girl."

Bill continued, "So Susie comes home with a signed photograph of this year's Rodeo Queen and a hair-brained scheme for a mounted drill team in the parade -- sequined cowboy hats, silk neckerchiefs, flowing banners, the whole nine yards. Scaled down, of course. There're only three horses in Two Sloughs: Susie's old nag, Sally Martin's miserable crow bait and my Barbara's well-mannered quarter horse."

The rest of the counter hooted. "Sold for $50 off a glue factory lot," said Dan Martin.

"I vetoed banners on long poles right off the bat." Bill ignored Dan. "Somebody would've gotten her eye poked out, sure as I'm sitting here. They were fresh out of sequined hats at Lim Kee Dry Goods, but Barbara conned her mother into making them matching flowing silk neckerchiefs, out of our bathroom curtains. The girls painted the scarves with stars and stripes and glued glitter around the edges...."

"We were up to our.... in glue and glitter, I can tell you," chimed in Joe Scoleri.

Ruth settled onto her stool. This was going to be a good one. The Fourth of July Parade was always a big event in Two Sloughs. It coincided with the beginning of pear picking, the busiest time of the year, so preparations were slap-dash but elaborate -- lots of last-minute poster paint and scotch tape and red, white and blue crepe paper. The Two Sloughs Volunteer Fire Department was more or less in charge. The parade started at about ten in the morning and circled the middle block of Lambert Tract twice or three times, depending on how long the parade turned out to be and how hot it was, and ended in front of the firehouse, where the firemen handed out popsicles to all the kids. Apparently Ruth had missed a lulu this year.

"I said the mounted drill team had better bring up the rear of the parade," said Dan Martin, "as far away as possible from the fire engines."

Ben Heimann leaned down the counter, "I was driving one of the fire engines, leading the parade, loaded with little kids and firemen, lights flashing, sirens blaring, the whole works. Charlene's Brownie Troop marched behind the fire engines this year. Then came the tricycles and bicycles. You know, red, white and blue crepe paper wound in their spokes, little American flags stuck to their handlebars."

"Were there floats this year?" Ruth asked. There were always a couple of family floats, last-minute, home made affairs set up on pear trailers, pulled by tractors.

"Three," Harvey Lemmon said. "Hendersons had George Washington crossing the Delaware in a refrigerator carton."

Ike laughed. "The Gianninis and their cousins mounted Lorraine Giannini as a kind of wobbly Statue of Liberty, all draped in bed sheets, holding up an oleander torch. With all the Giannini cousins and little brothers skulking around her feet as the Huddled Masses, looking hot as hell."

"And you know the Pratts," Harvey said. "They always have some exotic theme because they've got that clump of pampas grass in their back yard."

Apparently the Pratts joined the parade late, and their poster paint signs smeared. None of the men was sure, even Bill Pratt, "Something about Cleopatra," he thought.

"So last come the horses," Joe Scoleri said, "suspicious, skeedadling sideways. Those three girls must have practiced 100 hours riding three abreast, but Martin's horse Pansy was crow-hopping ten yards to the rear, loaded for bear."

Everybody knew Pansy, even Ruth. Pansy was a great tub of a pinto mare who had been handed down from little girl to little girl over the years. Pansy had earned a reputation around town for hysteria.

Ben Heimann continued, "So the second time around the block, as we get back to the firehouse corner where most of the spectators stand and poor Sally Martin's struggling to get Pansy up into line, Lionel Noble rides by on his bike and tosses a string of firecrackers a little too close to Pansy's tail...."

The men were all laughing now.

"Pansy shoots off like some damned Roman candle," Ike said, illustrating with his spatula, "bolts right past the other two horses, through the tricycles, up onto the sidewalk, straight along those little clumps of front lawn, clompety clomp, churning up grass like a rototiller, scattering spectators, lawn chairs..."

"Sally Martin's cowboy hat flies off," said Bill Kramer. "She's shrieking and yanking on the reins and swearing at Lionel. Pansy picks up speed. We all take off after her, along with about a dozen boys on decorated bikes and all the dogs on the street, both the decorated dogs and the undecorated ones, all barking.

"Pansy tries to jump our camellia bush but misses," continued Bill. "Then she veers off through the McClatchy's petunia bed, cuts through a couple of back yards, (By now she's dragging the McClatchy's clothes line, too,) rounds the corner and runs smack into the front of the parade turning the corner from the opposite direction."

"That's me," says Ben Heimann, "on the lead engine. I got my lights flashing and my sirens blaring. That did it. By now, that old Pansy's wild-eyed, snorting, foaming at the mouth. She cuts right, heads out of town, and sends Sally sailing straight over into the Lemmon's Early Girl tomatoes, which are being irrigated."

By now Ruth was laughing so hard she couldn't speak, much less finish her glazed doughnut. Tears were rolling down her cheeks.

"Somebody's got to come up with a way to get girls through puberty without the aid of horses," Dan Martin said. "I'm buyin' the coffee."

That day after school, Jimmy Martin stood at the open door of Miss Hardy's office. She looked up startled, feeling those serious eyes focused on her. "Hi Jimmy, come in." Jimmy edged just inside the dark office trying to look invisible, plucking up his courage. Miss Hardy pretended to go on reading the papers in front of her, so as not to spook him. "Anything I can do for you?" she asked.

Jimmy squirmed, "Are you really gonna keep Lionel's BB gun for a whole month?"

Ruth looked up at the skinny child standing scared spitless before her on behalf of his friend.

"Jimmy, the thing is, trouble has a way of getting out of hand when there's a gun involved. You know what I mean? It's like those Fourth of July firecrackers times ten, times a thousand."

"Pansy is a dumb horse," Jimmy said with conviction.

Ruth studied her blotter, trying to compose her face. She had heard pretty much the same assessment at Ike's that very morning. "The point is, guns are big trouble."

"Yes, ma'am. I could keep an eye on him."

"Thanks, Jimmy. I'll have a talk with...."

"See, we got to practice," Jimmy interrupted urgently, taking two steps into the room, "Cause..."

Ruth waited.

"My Dad's going to take me hunting.... Pheasant...." Despair filled his voice, "But not 'til I'm ready." He ducked his head down and twisted his right foot around behind his left leg, scratching the back of his ankle.

"Not 'til you're ready, huh? Well, that's probably a good idea," said Miss Hardy sympathetically.

"Yeah," Jimmy thrust both hands in his pockets. "Seems like I'll never be ready for anything."

"You will be, Jimmy. You will be. Tell you what. I'll have a talk with Lionel. Maybe we can work something out. But I can't promise anything. Lionel doesn't always want to talk. And he doesn't always listen either. That's a problem."

Jimmy shrugged, "Maybe it's 'cause you ain't his mom."

"Aren't."

"Aren't. He doesn't have one," Jimmy said. "A mom."

"Yes, well, there's not much I can do about that, is there?"

"No."

"Jimmy, whether you've got no mom or three moms, when you get to be eleven you've got to start taking some responsibility for yourself. Maybe that's what your Dad means by 'being ready.'"

Jimmy sighed.

Ruth put her papers in her top drawer. "You know what this day calls for? One of Freddy's Ice Cream Sundaes. Care to join me?"

"Really?"

"Really. Let's get out of here."

Ruth always tried to balance her punishments with some reward. But in Jimmy's case she was also honoring courage and loyalty to his friend. She was offering a little compensation, too. Having Sally Martin as a big sister couldn't be easy. And being eleven is always tough. This was a special occasion, and, in Ruth's opinion, the Two Sloughs Pharmacy and Soda Fountain came about as close to glamour as Two Sloughs got.

The Two Sloughs Pharmacy sat up on top of the levee facing the river. The outside of the building looked like all the rest of the store fronts in Two Sloughs, old and in need of paint. The Breams owned them all. The only embellishment outside was a yellow banksia rose that blanketed the whole sunny side of the building, trailing off down behind the levee. But inside the store gleamed. Ruth could never get over it. Freddy Noble was a meticulous pharmacist, and the back of the store, which the public never saw, was a model of pharmaceutical order. His pharmacist's smock was always spotlessly white, freshly starched. The stand up collar and the tunic buttons down the right front panel looked nearly dashing on Freddy somehow. And Freddy's soda fountain made Ruth laugh with pleasure just to look at it. It was pure glitz, really. She thought there was probably more chrome on Freddy's soda fountain than in all the rest of Two Sloughs put together, including Bill Pratt's Ford dealership. A long mirror stretched the length of the soda fountain so that she and Jimmy could perch up on two of the six black leatherette revolving stools and see all the chromed syrup dispensers and the chromed soda water squirter and the chromed milk shake mixer on the green melamine stand, and then see them all reflected again in the mirror. The tops of the doors of the ice cream freezer were chrome, too, and hinged in the center. When Freddy leaned over and opened one to scoop out a cone, and the overhead lights shone down on him, the flash of chrome nearly blinded them.

When Freddy formulated prescriptions, he was strictly business. All Ruth could see was the top of his head bent over behind his partition. Jimmy couldn't see him at all. Mrs. Lemmon ran interference for him behind the cash register. Mrs. Lemmon could serve up a Coca-Cola, too, two squirts with the heel of her hand into the curvaceous glass and then a quick splash of soda and a stir with a long spoon. But when it came to ice cream, it seemed to Ruth it was all show business, and Freddy was the star of the show. Freddy had enough of a sense of humor to appreciate the situation. Ruth knew that Freddy's mother had wanted Freddy to be a doctor. Freddy had wanted to be a star of musical comedies. As it turned out, Freddy was too shy and the money was too scarce for either of their pipe dreams, so they compromised: Freddy became a pharmacist.

But when Freddy stepped up behind the soda fountain at the front of the pharmacy, banked by all that chrome and the mirror and the lights, Ruth could almost hear the pit orchestra begin to play. He could make a hot fudge sundae sing, a dipper of hot fudge swirled all around the bottom of the fluted glass, then two enormous scoops of ice cream clapped together so that they stood tall in the glass, then a cascade of chocolate fudge that trilled down the ice cream and pooled around the top of the glass. Then Freddy flipped all his little chrome toppings containers open, all at once, with the flick of his wrist, and he lavished the sundae with gobs of whipped cream and sprinkles of nuts and maraschino cherries so red they screamed, "eat me." Ruth and Jimmy watched as Freddy set a paper lace doily on a saucer. Carefully balancing so that not a drop spilled, he placed that opulent glass on the saucer and presented it to Jimmy. Then he turned with a flourish, "And you, Miss, what may I get for you?"

"Oh, the same, Freddy," laughed Ruth. "Encore!"

Ruth stopped by on Friday after school to see Tosh at his shoe repair shop in Japan Town. His building, like all the others in Japan Town, was owned by the Breams. Any paint on the buildings had flaked away long ago. To Ruth, the storefronts looked hunkered down behind the levee, below the pharmacy and the grocery and the bank. Bare bones of buildings, they held one another up along the narrow streets, their windows vacant, their railings broken. Tosh's shop backed right up against the levee so that it was deep and narrow, and the only light came in through the front window. Tosh had set up his workbench under the window. Ruth perched in a crooked chair by the door. She was in her stocking feet although the floor was rough planked and full of splinters.

"You're hard on your shoes, Miss Hardy." Tosh wore his thick leather apron. His mouth was full of nails.

"It's all that beating time to the music, Tosh. Football season is the hardest on 'em, though. I go through a set of heels every football season."

"And another set for baseball," Tosh said. He shook his head and pried off the old flattened heels as they talked.

"Doc says there's talk of the Breams raising rents over here."

"We've already gotten the notice. January 1. Nice New Year's present, huh?"

"Oh, brother," Ruth said.

"Don't worry, it's not our New Year," Tosh said wryly. He tapped his hammer a few times, intent on his work, "Maybe he wants to get rid of us."

"Why would he want to do that, Tosh?"

"Yeah," Tosh laughed bitterly. Who else but 'Japs' would live in these dumps."

If you were one of my students, I'd keep you after school for using that word," said Ruth gently.

"I didn't invent it," said Tosh. Ever notice how we're always called 'Japs,' even though we're U.S. citizens, even though our kids have never even seen Japan?"

"Ever notice how the Gianninis are called 'Wops' and the Scoleris are called 'Portagee'?" Ruth asked. "Heck, the Germans have six different names, none of 'em complimentary."

"Yeah, but they weren't locked up. We look different. They can pick us out of a crowd."

"I don't defend them, Tosh, but the war hasn't been over very long. There are some pretty fresh scars. Anyway, Old Man Bream's not chasing away my best trumpet player, or my best math student, either. Did you hear your niece got a perfect score on the state math test? The District called to see if we'd made a mistake. Bream's not getting rid of you without a fight. This town won't let him."

"Maybe the town agrees with him." Tosh was suddenly very intent on the heel of Ruth's shoe.

Ruth looked at him carefully. The men Tosh's age had taken Relocation Camp the hardest. They had lost their businesses and their savings, but those could be rebuilt. Their pride was irreparably damaged. Their manhood seemed to have been wounded somehow. Tosh's shoulders rounded in a defeated way; his gaze was downward.

"Funny thing," Tosh muttered, "I just finished teaching a citizenship class here in Japan Town, so they can all apply for citizenship if they ever get the chance. And so the citizens can re-register to vote. You know, land of the free, home of the brave, Bill of Rights.... I skip the Oriental Exclusion Acts. There're too many of them." Tosh was giving her shoe one hell of a pounding. "Those old grandmothers are all busting a gut trying to learn to sign their names in English." He sat back and smiled, "They do it like calligraphy: 'Over the mountain; into the valley.' That's how you teach calligraphy. It doesn't mean a thing to them otherwise."

"More power to them," said Ruth. She made a mental note to incorporate some calligraphy techniques in the third grade penmanship lessons (Over the mountain; into the valley.) "Tosh, this town is as full of meanness and hurt and prejudice as the next one. But you've been good neighbors. The town knows it. They'll be on your side in this one." Ruth paid for her heels and went home wondering if what she had said was true. Tosh wondered the same thing.

Well, somebody had to talk to Old Man Bream. But when Ruth dropped in at Ike's the next morning, she didn't get any takers. There was a long silence, long even for Ike's, after she explained the problem, a lot of studious examination of coffee mugs.

"Be careful of that guy, Ruth," Harvey Lemmon said finally.

"These people didn't have anything to do with the Coral Sea. We can't let Bream get away with this," Ruth said. "These families have nowhere else to go. They'll have to pay it. And it's high way robbery."

"Too many Japs around any...." Ben Heimann grumbled.

Ben had lost a son on Guam. Every man in Ike's knew that.

"Easy, Ben," Harvey Lemmon cut him off. Harvey had landed on Iwo Jima. Everybody knew that, too.

"It wouldn't be the first time Bream's robbed...." Bill Pratt's voice trailed off. He didn't even try to finish his sentence.

"Ruth, the guy's mean," Dan Martin said. "My dad found out the hard way. Nearly lost our land one time because of Bream."

"Then you got that grandson..." Harvey muttered.

Ruth was dumfounded. Fear seemed to coat the men's tongues. Their voices were thick with warning. These were guys who'd fought at Guadacanal, at Anzio, some of them. None of them cowards. For the first time she could remember, the silence at Ike's was uncomfortable. Even Ike wouldn't look her in the eye.

Ruth stood up, "Well, I've got nothing to lose. $300 in the bank, is all. I'll go myself."

"Ruth," Ike said, "Do me a favor. Sleep on it. Don't stir up trouble you can't put a lid on."

Ruth knew Mr. Bream, but she'd never been to visit him in his apartment above the bank. She was so uneasy after the men's warnings, so intent on her errand the next morning that details of her visit came to her only later when she got home and tried to piece together what had happened.

She'd forgotten about Jenny, Mr. Bream's older maiden sister, who lived with him. When Ruth rang the doorbell, one of the windows above the bank's preposterous Ionic columns opened, and Jenny stuck her head out.

"What in hell do you want?" she yelled.

"I'd like to speak to Mr. Bream. Bank business," Ruth said, aware that everybody on the street was looking at Jenny, then at Ruth and then back at Jenny, wondering if Jenny was wearing underpants today. Jenny was 82 years old and slightly cross-eyed. Her chief interests were collecting rubber bands and doing yoga exercises. Jenny sorted her rubber bands according to width, length and color. She kept them on the carved knobs of the stair posts leading up to their second floor apartment so that the stair railing bulged with bulbous, obscene rubber-clad posts. But Ruth was only vaguely aware of the rubber bands or the boxes of used Christmas wrapping paper that cluttered the narrow staircase. The smells of cat and cigarette and ripe garbage grew stronger as she ascended. At the top of the stairs, on a cramped landing, Ruth came face to face with the belly of a mammoth mahogany grandfather clock. The clock towered over Ruth, nearly black, with clawed feet splayed out to the sides, corpulent, twisted columns that rose up the clock like the front legs of some prize bull to a series of graduated cornices, gilded capitols, feather moldings and gilded curlicues, all black and greasy and hung with cobwebs. Ruth hesitated on the landing, confused by the presence of this Victorian monster. Suddenly the beast belched the Westminster Chimes, out of time, out of tune, and then the hour, ten o'clock. Ruth could hear Jenny still leaning out the front window yelling at her, "Don't come around here trying to collect for anything. Go away. We're busy."

Ruth entered the living room of the apartment slightly winded by the stairs and the assault from the clock. Only later did she remember the massive dark Victorian furniture that seemed to take up all the walls. Had the ceiling been particularly low, or was the furniture of such gigantic scale? It felt shoved in somehow, as if it had been a tight squeeze and they maybe had to remove a top knot or finial here and there to cram it all in. A stout legged mahogany dining table was pushed up next to the front windows. The top was covered with scuffed oilcloth and a dozen open jars and a can of condensed milk. In the center of the table stood a silver framed portrait of a handsome young man in his Air Force uniform. Mr. Bream sat at one end of the table in suit and tie clutching a fly swatter. As Ruth entered the room, the fly swatter came down on the oilcloth with a smack. Several flies buzzed frantically over the table aiming for the jam jars. Mr. Bream swatted again. "Ha!" he said, his eyes still fixed upon the circling flies. "What do you want?"

"Good morning," Ruth said, more hoarsely than she would have liked.

"Hmmmph," Bream said and swatted angrily at the table in front of Ruth. Ruth hadn't seen a fly alight there. She didn't jump, but she was losing her concentration fast. Jenny was getting down on her hands and knees.

"Dear God, let her have her underpants on," thought Ruth. The whole town knew that Jenny liked to show off her yoga to guests. Her finale was standing on her head, which she did well for an 82-year-old. She was strong, limber for 82, but her short-term memory was failing her. She sometimes forgot to wear underpants, which made for pretty memorable yoga demonstrations. She sat on the floor now, grunting, with her legs crossed and her neck extended at a cockeyed angle that accentuated her crossed eyes.

The floor of the living room was piled with stacks of yellowed Wall Street Journals wrapped in string. Bream swatted again, narrowly missing the ashtray full of cigarette butts and the open can of condensed milk in front of him. "Ha," he said triumphantly.

"I want to talk to you about the rents in Japan Town," Ruth said, trying to gather her wits together.

"Why?" demanded Bream as he studied the flies circling the open jam jars on the table. " God Damned Japs."

That made Ruth mad, "Because the war's over. Because I think they're too high, that's why." She was warming to her task.

"I'm about to raise them."

"If you do, you'll lose every tenant you've got. They can't pay any more. And I'll lose half my school."

"So that's it! The state pays you by the head, do they? Well, Missy, that's your look-out." Smack! "A god-damned bounty hunter's what you are." Bream chuckled, "Cramming your school with Japs. In it for the money."

Ruth felt her jaw drop. She caught her breath. She could feel the color rising in her face, "Mr. Bream, if you raise those rents, I'll report every health code and sanitation code and safety code violation I can dig up down there. I'll get Clarence Henderson to go over the wiring. I'll get Doc involved. I'll go to the county..."

Swap! A fly lay splattered on the oilcloth. "You think you've got more clout in this county than I do, Missy? You think I couldn't yank Clarence Henderson's mortgage out from under him tomorrow? You think Doc isn't up to his ass in debt to me with that office of his and his house, too. Hell, that X-ray machine cost him...." Swat! "You mind your own business, Missy, or you'll find yourself with a real ornery school board on your hands all of a sudden."

"You couldn't...."

Bream looked her in the eye then, a nasty, narrow glare, "Don't tempt me, girl, don't tempt me."

It was only later, after she was out in the fresh air, that Ruth remembered Jenny upside down in the corner, two withered legs sticking up out of a pair of grimy pink underclothes.

Bill Pratt had stopped telling jokes at Ike's cafe. The men all noticed it. They didn't miss the jokes. Hell, they were terrible jokes, car salesman jokes, pointless, dirty, went on forever. But Bill was a good storyteller, and he loved to tell a story. He'd laugh 'til tears came to his eyes, 'til you had to laugh at him or with him, one or the other. Lately he'd come into Ike's in the morning and just sit at the counter nursing his coffee, never say a word.

Dan Martin sat down next to him one day about a month after school started, "How's Mavis, Bill?" he asked gently. "Heard things weren't so good."

Bill rested his head in his hand, "They're worse than that," he said.

"Jesus," Ben Heimann said.

There was a sympathetic mumble all along the counter.

"She's hurtin'," Bill said, "and there's nothin' I can do to help her. Nothin'."

Ike refilled his cup.

"Sometimes I can't stand to watch it. It's wearing us all out."

"You can say that again," said Larry Jepsen glumly.

Nobody moved. They all smelled trouble. In the long silence that followed the men took apart Larry Jepsen's comment word by word, ("You can say that again,") as if the comment were a two-cycle engine that wasn't catching, as if they could dismantle it, maybe clean out the air filter, retard the spark, get to the bottom of the problem. "You can say that again," Larry had said. Was Charlene Jepsen worn out by Mavis's illness? She was Mavis's best friend. Was Charlene sick herself? Her car had been at Doc's a lot lately. Was something else the matter? Ike made a round with his rag, wiping the counter, straightening the salt and peppers, the ketchup bottles, as if neatness might help.

At that moment Elsie Phipps, the town postmistress, bustled into the strained silence at Ike's so excited she didn't even feel it, didn't catch the intent expressions on the men's faces. She waved a fat envelope for Louie Riccetti. "It's registered, Louie. I think it might be important. Open it."

Louie's face turned red. He hunched further over his cup of coffee. "Thanks, Elsie. I'll get to it later."

"But, Louie," said Elsie, "It's from Washington D.C. I think it might be about that corn growing contest."

"Yeah, well, we'll see," Louie said. "Holy Mother, I'm late already," he said, fished out a quarter from his pocket, left it on the counter, grabbed his rolled up sports section and the letter. "Thanks, Elsie," he said again. The screen door banged behind him.

Nobody said a word for a minute or two.

"Oh, dear," Elsie said, "I hope I didn't...."

"Sit down, Elsie. Coffee?" Ike said.

"It's just that I thought...." Elsie said miserably.

"It's not your fault, Elsie," Tony Riccetti said. "You didn't know." He hesitated, looking at his coffee. Tony was the youngest man at the counter, in his early twenties, a big burly kid with black hair and eyebrows that nearly met across his brow. He looked up fiercely, "If this ever gets out, I'll drown the guy responsible in the nearest ditch. Now I mean it." He looked down the row of faces at the counter, then back at his coffee mug. "You see, the thing is, Uncle Louie can't read."

"What?"

"Go on."

"Why, he reads the sports section of the SACRAMENTO BEE every morning of his life, sitting right here at my counter," Ike said.

"He <u>looks</u> at the sports section," Tony corrected him. He paused. "He's real touchy about this."

"But his brother Joe's a C.P.A. Teresa's a librarian, for Christ sake!"

"Louie was the oldest. Their dad was already sick when they got over here. Louie had to quit school and go to work. He just never got the chance to go back. Then it got too embarrassing, and well...." Tony leaned his elbows on the counter and rubbed the back of his neck, "He was sore at me for even entering him in that corn growing contest. Told me if he did win the damned thing, he wouldn't go back for it. He said they might ask him to read something."

Nobody budged. Every man there sat scouring his memory for signs they should have picked up, tight spots they might have put Louie in, not knowing. Even Ike sat down, on the stool nearest the door, by the cash register.

"We got to do something," said Ike.

"This is a national big deal award. If he did win this thing it'd be the biggest goddamn award anybody in Two Sloughs ever got."

"Oughta be. Louie is the best goddamned farmer in Two Sloughs."

"And the nicest," chimed in Elsie. "Isn't one of us doesn't owe him a favor. When I think of all the sweet corn and the beefsteak tomatoes he's brought by my mother's...."

"Couldn't his brother Joe go with him, or one of his nephews?"

"He won't do it, I tell you," said Tony.

"Then we got to teach him to read," said Harvey Lemmon. "We got time. Isn't that awards deal usually in late January, February?"

"He's gonna kill me," Tony moaned.

"Well then, the first thing is we've got to make a pact not to let this out of this room." Dan Martin said. "The second thing is we've got to put Ruth Hardy on it."

"He'd rather die than admit it to Miss Hardy. He's scared to death of that woman," Tony said.

"Dan's right," said Freddy Noble. "Ruth'll figure out a way. She'll do it too. She's not as hard-boiled as she looks."

"Don't be so sure, Freddy," Harvey Lemmon said, "but if anybody can do it, she can."

"All right," said Tony miserably, "I'll go talk to her." Tony's last run-in with Miss Hardy had been eight years back when he played first chair, first trumpet. She'd yanked him up by his hair every day for four solid weeks before the state band competition because he was playing flat. His head ached just thinking about her. But they had won the god damned thing, taken second prize, away from a lot of fancy bands with uniforms and drum majors and school busses to drive them in. Yeah, he'd go talk to Miss Hardy. "But if nothing comes of this, I don't ever want to hear another word about it," Tony said, "not one word." And he walked out.

"That kid's coming along," said Harvey.

A week later, Louie stopped by Ruth's house one evening with an armful of sweet corn. Ruth wasn't ready for him. She'd racked her brain trying to figure out how to approach Louie's reading problem ever since Tony had come by the house asking for her help, refusing to come inside ("I've been plowing,") twisting the pickets on her fence out front 'til she thought he'd break them off one by one like match sticks. Tony had warned her that Louie would be touchy about this. She and Louie had never been close. He'd been generous to her, but reserved. Ruth had always assumed he was protecting his bachelor status. Obviously there'd been more to it.

She gathered the sweet corn up in her arms as if it were a newborn, "Louie, I wait all year for this. It's a meal in itself."

"It's good for you Ruth. Keep your strength up."

"Louie," Ruth shifted uncomfortably. "I have a favor to ask you."

"Sure, Ruth."

"It's kind of embarrassing. You got time to come in for a minute?" Ruth lovingly put the ears of corn on the drain board, and they sat down at the kitchen table. Louie fidgeted with his John Deere cap in front of him on the table, creasing the bill with his thumb and forefinger. Ruth sighed, "The truth is, I've never told a soul in Two Sloughs about this. The truth is, I wouldn't even have had the courage to tell you except.... I mean if this ever got out.... If Lionel Noble ever got hold of this...."

"Ruth, for pity sakes...." Louie could see she was suffering.

"Louie, I'm scared of rats." She blurted it out.

"What?" Louie looked at her incredulously.

"I mean, scared to death of 'em. Have been all my life. I mean, nightmares, that kind of thing. I know it sounds dumb, but I have this lousy terror of them." She couldn't believe she was admitting this to Louie. Only desperation would have made her admit it to anybody. "Every year about this time I start to worry about them getting into the house. Once the rains come and this end of the island gets wet, the rats start looking for a place to hide." She shuddered, "Louie, I haven't been inside that shed out back for two years, I'm so afraid of them. I wouldn't have mentioned it, even to you, except your nephew Tony came by the other day. He's worried you wouldn't go to Washington D.C. to accept that prize from the President if you won it. He says what's stopping you is you can't read very well."

She saw Louie flinch, saw him set his jaw, "Louie, if you'd help me with the rats..." She straightened up, "and keep it quiet, mind you, I could teach you to read in no time. Louie, I can't stand another winter with these rats."

Ruth had tears in her eyes. This was no act. The thought of opening the shed door, the scurrying sounds, the sight of a long, naked tail disappearing behind a box made her shiver.

"Ruth, you put those rats right out of your mind. I'll set some traps tonight before I leave, and I'll check them, so don't you give 'em a thought. And I'll get to that shed of yours someday next week when I got the time. As for the other, Tony had no business mentioning it...."

"Louie, I'd never...."

"I know you wouldn't Ruth. And this rat thing is strictly between us, you and me. But that corn contest is just a bunch of politicians looking for some hands to shake. I don't want any part of it."

Ruth was losing him. He stood up, bunched his shoulders, turned away. She'd seen a hundred first grade boys do the same thing: I can't do it, and I don't care, and I don't want to talk about it. "Louie," she said desperately, "I'm sure I could help you with this reading business. There are a few tricks...."

"I get by all right." He put his cap on, headed for the kitchen door.

"I know you do, but the thing is this rat business is too important to me." Tears were running down her cheeks. She didn't care. She'd started out to trick Louie and caught herself up instead. She'd let down her guard to this generous, gentle man, and he'd responded to her. "Please Louie, I want to pay you back some way, and this is about the only thing I know how to do." She sniffled. "Unless you want to learn to play the trumpet."

Louie laughed. He turned around, leaned against the kitchen door and laughed. "O.K. Ruth," he said, "we'll give it a shot."

"But not a word to anybody," pleaded Ruth.

Louie patted her hand, "I know, little one. I feel that way about this god-damned reading thing."

Ruth stopped crying, "Great, she said, "then it's a deal? Shake on it?"

All fall Louie Riccetti showed up promptly at 7:00 Tuesday and Thursday nights at Miss Hardy's door with an armful of corn or a box of tomatoes or some green peppers from his garden. Eventually somebody noticed his pickup parked in front of Ruth's door so often.

"Do you think there's something going on?" Josephine Lemmon asked her husband.

"No," said Harvey.

October

One Saturday morning in October Dan Martin's rusty pickup jolted along a dirt road back of the house. Dan drove, both hands on the wheel, elbows out, legs spread, as if he were accustomed to sitting a horse with a bum gait. His eyes were on the ditch beside him. The sun was already up, a heavy sun sunk low along the sky. It turned the corn stubble brassy. Pheasant season, when the corn was off and sold, and whatever could go wrong had already gone wrong and getting up at five in the morning wouldn't help it.

Jimmy bounced up and down beside his father on the bench seat of the pickup. He looked out at the dirt road that shimmered damp and brown before them, cross-rutted, patterned like the long tail feathers of a cock pheasant. The whole morning looked golden to him, pheasant colored -- the corn stubble, the cinnamon red weeds hung with shining spider webs, the iridescent puddles along the road. It seemed to him he'd waited eleven years for this golden morning, the morning of his first hunt. He sat close to his door, twiddling the knob of the window crank.

"Don't do that, son. You'll twist it off."

Jimmy stopped. His sideways glance caught the sharp edge of his father's face. Jimmy's chin sank into his jacket collar. He leaned back against the seat, taking up very little room. He was eleven. Seemed like no matter what he did, he couldn't get older. Suddenly he was full of dread. What if he wounded a bird and couldn't wring its neck? He'd watched his father do it, grab that scarlet head, a flick of the wrist, almost casual, and the bird was dead. But what if the bird struggled in his hands, opened its golden eye, flapped its wings. Jimmy had seen them do that.

What if, after all this time of waiting, he couldn't hit one? What if he missed?

Dan wished he hadn't had to start out that way. But the pickup was falling apart quick enough by itself. They were both nervous. He pulled up at the far end of the corn stubble. "Well, you gonna get out? Or sit there waiting for the pheasant to come to you?" He had meant that to be a joke.

Jimmy looked at him with dull, confused eyes.

"Now, Jimmy," Dan said, "you've been giving those tin cans hell back behind the shed...." Don't baby him, Dan thought. He slammed his door and continued jovially, "Let's see how you do when these old daddy pheasant come exploding out of the stubble, all whirr and feathers." Dan let his dog out of the back of the pickup and sat with the boy on the tailgate, trying to sort out his son's sudden sullenness. Jimmy had been so excited about his first pheasant hunt that he couldn't finish his dinner last night, couldn't touch his breakfast. He hadn't talked about anything else for weeks.

Dan put his arm around the boy. What he wanted to say was, "I remember my first hunt. I was scared spitless, too. At least you don't have your grandfather stalking off into the corn ahead of you, never once looking back, not once. You'll be O.K.," he wanted to say to his son. "I won't let you fail."

But a man has to grow up sometime. Can't coddle him. What Dan said was, "You understand why we only shoot cocks?" Matter-of-factly, man to man. "Every hen out there means four, maybe six chicks next spring. You understand that."

"Yeah," Jimmy muttered into his collar.

Dan patted his bottom, "Well, tie your bootlace, and come on."

Dan handed the boy his .410 shotgun. "Now, you be careful, hear? Stay even with me and don't swing around on me. These old devils can scare the daylights out of you."

Dan's dog, a broad-chested Irish setter, danced around his master, whining, drooling.

Jimmy slouched silently against the side of the pickup looking down at his gun, his finger tracing the fine lines along the side of the barrel. He'd been waiting for this morning his whole life long, the morning of his first hunt. Suddenly, he dreaded it. He couldn't breathe. The end of his gun barrel grazed the stubble.

Dan was irritated by the boy's lack of enthusiasm. "Watch it," he snapped. "You'll get mud in the barrel. Don't let your gun drag like that," He said and walked off.

Jimmy trudged after him, trying to keep up, squinting as if the whole world blinded him, as if he looked at the world through the glint along the barrel of his gun. He squinted, rubbed his nose, fumbled the shells in his jacket pocket. The stubble came up nearly to his knees, thick stalks hacked sharp by the harvester. They hurt his shins. He watched his father stride along. The dog raced back and forth across the field, nose stretched out, tail streaming.

The dog stopped, forged on the golden field, front leg cocked, nose down, tail rigid.

"Now, easy, Jimmy. I'll kick it up. Ready? Don't shoot till I say."

A roar of wings shook the earth beneath Jimmy's feet, rent the stubble, shattered the sky. Jimmy staggered, tripped, raised his gun, shot.

"No," Dan shouted. "No, no. Hen."

The dog raced out, but the hen rose and flew straight up the field, dipping down behind the ditch. Dan whistled the dog back. Jimmy broke his gun and picked the empty shell out of the barrel, all thumbs, nearly gagging on the acrid smell of the gunpowder. He put the empty shell in his other pocket, took a new shell, placed it in the chamber, fingers shaking, snapped the gun shut, slid the safety up. He didn't look at the dog or at his father.

Dan watched him, helpless, wondering if the boy was going to throw up. They walked on side by side while Dan thought of things he might say. The field was still again, except for the red dog working out ahead of them.

"Well, that's over with. The first one always knocks you for a loop," Dan said. "OK, this time take a bead on him, but wait for me to call it."

Again the dog quivered like an arrow shot into a straw target. Dan kicked the bird out, jumped back. "Shoot," he shouted. "Shoot!"

Again the dog leaped out at the sound of the shot. Dan whistled him back. "That wasn't bad," he said. "You shot behind him, was all."

Jimmy rubbed his shoulder, then tugged at his jacket. Dan pretended not to notice, pretended everything was fine, even the weather, though they needed more rain. Nothing you can do about the weather, so why talk about it all the time.

They were nearly at the other end of the field. Jimmy had shot at a hen and four cocks. Clean misses.

Every afternoon since school started, Jimmy had practiced with the cans. He and Lionel had set them against the shed. Sometimes his father would come by to throw a couple into the air for him. He could hit a can. Why couldn't he hit a pheasant? They were bigger. They were huge. He'd cleaned his shotgun a dozen times since September, till his room smelled of Hoppe's #9 solvent from the rags he kept in a coffee can beside his bed. He'd waited so long.

"If you're not ready now, you never will be," his father had said.

"Move up," Dan said. "They'll start coming out fast now. They've been sneaking along ahead of us. They'll make a break for it now."

Jimmy knew this was his last chance. He had to hit one now. Two hens whirled off to the right and down behind the cattails. A cock sprang straight into the sun, blinding him in his gun's glare. The dog rushed in on another cock before Jimmy could reload his single barrel. He wrestled with his gun while the sound of the birds exploded in his head.

The dog stared at him, discouraged, then brushed right by him, ignored him. Jimmy kicked the dog savagely. The dog yelped and fell away.

"Stop that," roared Dan. "Stop it." He snatched his son by the collar. "Don't you ever let me catch you kicking a dog again. Hear me? Any dog. What's the matter with you?"

The dog circled, slunk around behind Dan. Dan rolled a dirt clod over with his boot, eyed the boy, put his free arm around him. Jimmy turned away.

"It's not easy. Nobody said it was easy, Honey." Dan's voice was cracked and rusty. "It takes time. You got to work at it."

Jimmy raised his chin, shot his father a look of pure hate, right between the eyes, then pulled his chin back down, clenched his jaw, locked up his face.

Dan saw the look, kept silent, broke off a stalk along the ditch, examined it although he knew it was only Curly Dock, no-good weed. He turned back down the field. "Now we'll walk this side," he said. "The smart ones are all still in here. We only scared the hens and the silly youngsters." The word "youngsters" stuck in his throat, but he'd said it, so he let it go. "Now don't let your gun stop on you. Nice easy swing, like when I throw the cans." Jimmy was walking slack, dragging his feet through the stubble. "Silly youngsters, silly youngsters." The words shuffled around in his head.

"And be ready," Dan said irritably.

Again the dog froze on point, lunged, returned tail down. And again. The boy stood shuddering with anticipation like the dog, raised his .410, shot. His father stood tensed beside him, talking to him, willing the little pattern of shot to catch a wing, a back, hell, a tail feather.

As they neared the pickup, the dog took up a last point. Jimmy stumbled over toward the dog. Dan stood back. The boy kicked the bird up himself, followed it, shot, missed. As the cock wheeled off to the right, just at the apex of his rise, Dan shot. The bird tumbled, a heap of folded feathers, to the ground. Dan stared helplessly at the spot where the cock had fallen. "I think you winged that one," he said, embarrassed.

"No, I shot behind it."

"We'll try again tomorrow."

"Maybe."

The dog trotted up to his master, the bird limp in his mouth, iridescent color against the copper coat and the golden stubble.

"Good boy," the man said, scratched him around the ears and took the bird, swung it by the head to break its neck. He looked uncomfortably at his son. "Here," he tossed the pheasant to Jimmy. "Need a tail feather for your hat?"

"No."

Jimmy emptied his gun the way his father had shown him, pointed it up, shot it, put it on the rack along the rear window of the pickup.

They drove back down the dirt road along the ditch. Jimmy held the dead pheasant in his lap, stroking it, studying it, as if the bird knew all the answers.

That afternoon Lionel rode over on his bike. Jimmy was sitting on the back steps cleaning his shotgun.

"So, did ya plaster one?" Lionel asked.

"No."

"What happened?"

"I missed."

"None out there?"

"They were out there all right. I missed."

"All of 'em?"

Jimmy nodded.

"But we practiced."

"It's different," Jimmy said. "They come out roaring out. Like B-27 bombers. Right under your feet. Right in your face. They scare the piss out of you. I couldn't hit nothin'."

"Your dad mad?"

"Yeah."

"Wanna ride bikes?"

"No."

Lionel let his bike fall in the dirt and came to sit on the porch steps.

"Seems like I never do nothin' right when he's around," Jimmy said.

"Your dad?"

"Yeah. Seems like he hates me sometimes."

"Know what you mean. At least you've got a mom. What did she say?"

"You know, cheery Mom stuff. She doesn't get it."

If there was one thing that really drove Ruth crazy at Two Sloughs Elementary it was the mimeograph machine. Squeaking clarinets, sixth grade girls (who were the meanest creatures on God's green earth, in Ruth's opinion,) eraser fights -- all these plagues paled by comparison to the mimeograph machine. She had taken the cover off the machine and was down on her hands and knees with her Phillips screwdriver when the phone rang. She considered letting the darned thing ring, but the District Superintendent had an unnatural horror of not being able to contact his school principals at any moment, day or night. And if she didn't get it Nettie Crane at the phone company would come on the line to tell the Superintendent that Ruth was there, she'd made a local call, not five minutes ago, and Nettie would keep right on ringing her until she answered. Ruth spit the Phillips screws out of her mouth, nested them neatly on a ream of mimeograph paper. It struck her that if she was talking to the District Superintendent, she probably wasn't getting a thing done, but the Superintendent saw it differently. She sighed, crawled over to her desk, reached up and grabbed the receiver.

"Oh, hi, Joe.... Fine, thanks. What's up?" Joe Scoleri ran Joe's Bar and Restaurant. Joe bartended, cooked the baked beans with frankfurters and the beef stew that were on the menu every day (cooked them from scratch. Nothing canned.) He bar-b-qued the steaks he served on Saturday nights. He was a busy guy. He hadn't called to make small talk about Ruth's summer vacation.

"Ruth, Shirley Randolph's in here," Joe said, "She's pretty bad. Think you could send her kid over to pick her up?"

"Joe, I can't pull a kid out of class to send him to the local bar."

"Well, the thing is, I run a high class establishment," said Joe. "I can't have this kind of language in here."

Ruth smiled at the thought of Joe's high class establishment. "So the kid gets out of a spelling test because his mom's drunk?" she asked.

"You got a better idea? Ruth, he's the only one can handle her when she gets like this."

"But I...."

"Look, Ruth, I don't want to call the sheriff. He doesn't beat her if she doesn't get thrown in jail."

"Who doesn't beat her?"

"That old Filipino she lives with -- Ramirez."

"How'd she get mixed up with him?"

"Well, it's a roof over her head. And her kid's. He doesn't treat her too bad most of the time. Only if he has to go up to Sacramento and bail her out of jail. Look I got to go. She's getting ugly. Soon as you can, O.K.?"

Ruth sat on the floor of her office holding the telephone. They didn't put <u>this</u> in the principal's manual: Do not ring recess bell; no time to mimeograph arithmetic tests; too busy taxiing drunken mothers around town.

Ruth dropped by Miss Malberger's room on her way out to ask her to keep an eye on things, maybe get a little moral support, but Marian Malberger wasn't shocked when Ruth told her the situation.

"Yes," she'd said, "be sure Mrs. McClatchy gives him his homework assignments. He may not be able to come back."

Ten minutes later Ruth and Tommy Randolph were in Ruth's car on their way to Joe's Bar, over behind the Pharmacy.

"I'll take you and your mom home, Tommy. Where do you live?"

"Back of the Shelton Ranch with Francisco Ramirez. He's not my real father, though."

Ruth blinked. The little blonde kid beside her didn't look the least bit Filipino. "No?"

"Oh, no. My Dad was Thomas Walter Randolph from Virginia. Miss Malberger has it worked out that I'm related to Thomas Jefferson. He was from Virginia, too."

"That a fact?"

"Oh, yeah, that's probably why I'm good at trumpet. He was very musical, you know. Thomas Jefferson."

Luckily they were at Joe's Bar. Ruth was speechless.

Joe's Bar was pitch dark, except for the Christmas tree lights blinking behind the bar (which were a permanent decorative fixture, on a shelf above the liquor bottles, along with the cotton wool snow and the miniature wood village and the electric train) she had trouble adjusting her eyes to the dim light and the cigarette smoke. She heard Shirley Randolph before she saw her.

"Those misses... erable sons of bisshes....," Shirley wailed from her barstool in the corner. Fortunately, she had a wall beside her, the bar to lean on. Ruth tried to make out any similarity between her and Tommy, but her face had slid somehow. She was toothless. She wore a caved-in, damaged look that wasn't helped by the orange pancake make-up or the dyed red hair framing her fallen face. A dress of red and pink rayon roses hung on her, revealing a shriveled bosom.

"Men are mean bastards," she moaned, "dirty... gimmee a lil' shaser, Joe."

While Ruth stood at the door open-mouthed, Tommy went over to the bar, collected his mother's purse, put her arm around his shoulder, eased her off the barstool. "Come on, Ma," he said gently. Shirley looked up. Her face softened for a moment in a toothless smile of affection. "Tommy," she said, then her head dropped forward; the bitter taste of bourbon and defeat came back to her smeared lips. But she didn't resist him. Joe came around and supported her on the other side. Together they carried her out to Ruth's car and draped her across the back seat. Tommy put her filthy blue terry cloth mules and her purse in beside her, closed the door carefully, got in beside Ruth.

Joe handed Tommy a paper bag through the car window.

"She looks a lot better with her teeth in," Tommy explained, and Ruth realized her own face was giving her away. "She takes 'em out when she's going to be drinking so she won't lose em."

Ruth shut her own mouth and turned down Shelton Road.

"It'll be O.K. Francisco won't be home yet," Tommy said.

Ruth had the unsettled feeling this child was trying to reassure her. Shouldn't it be the other way around? Shouldn't she be saying soothing, sensible things?

"Dinner?" she asked, grasping at straws.

"Oh, we ain't much on dinner. And Joe always sends something home with her when he has to throw her out. We'll be fine." He looked out the window. "That's Miss Malberger's," he said. "See those sunflowers? I helped her plant them. She's no good with a shovel. I have to help her out quite a lot. In the garden and stuff. She can't hoe worth a damn either. She sure can cook, though." Tommy's stomach growled beside her on the front seat.

The Ramirez place was a quarter mile down the dirt road from Miss Malberger's. When they pulled up beside the carcasses of two cars, Tommy refused Ruth's offer to help him get his mother inside. "We ain't set up for company," he said, "but thanks anyway. It sure is easier getting her home with a car." He eased her out of the back seat and got her to the front step. Ruth left them sitting on the first step together.

"We ain't much on dinner." "We..." Ruth shook her head. "We" was a pronoun Ruth had little occasion to use herself. "We," the two of them, side by side on the front steps. How often did this child do this? Where did he get anything to eat? Did Francisco Ramirez beat him too? How had his mother strayed all the way from Virginia to this shack on the back levee? How could Tommy come out of that mess and play such a hell of a trumpet? She went back to her mimeograph machine feeling as if Tommy Randolph were older and wiser than she was.

Marian Malberger stuck her head in Ruth's office after school, "How'd it go with Tommy's mom?"

"She was pretty well plastered -- morose. Not too high on men. That kid's amazing with her. Joe says nobody else can handle her."

"He's a good kid."

"Marian, how much time does he spend at your place?"

Marian shifted uncomfortably. Teachers were not supposed to get mixed up in the children's home lives. District Policy. That was supposed to be left to the District Psychologist or the County Social Worker.

"Oh, a few odd jobs is all."

"And what about this Thomas Jefferson business?"

Marian turned huffy, "Well, it might very well be true. Jefferson did have Randolph relations, on his wife's side. Anyway it keeps the kids off his back. And it gives us something to work on during dinner."

"Dinner?"

"Well you don't think that old worn-out whore of a mother of his sits home baking pies and cookies, do you?" Marian snapped.

"One of Mr. Yee's girls?"

"No. Yee's girls are all Chinese. The house here in Two Sloughs uses white girls She worked here in town until she hit the bottle."

"So you feed him."

"Ruth," Marian pleaded, "he's a good kid. He hasn't got a chance in this world if somebody doesn't do a little something to help him."

"Marian Malberger, " Ruth said, "I think he's one lucky youngster." As she cranked her mimeograph machine, She thought of Marian and Tommy at the kitchen table. "Thomas Jefferson," she said to herself. "Thomas Jefferson." About the time she was feeling tough as a two penny nail, she ran up against one of these hardscrabble kids who hauled himself out of some shack on a back levee and learned to play the trumpet. It was the grin that got her. That gutsy little kid heaving his mother out of the car, all by himself, refusing her help. ("Thanks anyway. We ain't set up for company.") "We..." There's that pronoun again. And then the grin. She had a splitting headache.

She stopped on the way home for some aspirin. It was after 5:00. The lights had been turned off, but the door of the pharmacy was still open. The low sun streamed through the front windows. She caught Freddy Noble sitting on one of his soda fountain stools with his back to her, practicing his harmonica. He didn't hear her come in. She quietly hitched herself up onto a stool at the near end of the counter and listened. The joke around town was that Freddy would play his harmonica only when there was nobody to hear it. He was shy about playing in public. Ruth felt guilty sneaking up on him like this, but he played wonderfully. He'd taken off his pharmacist's tunic. His neck and shoulders surprised her. They were strong, muscular for such a slender man. His dark hair was carefully combed, but errant curls hid just behind his ears. Ruth didn't see Freddy often without his starched white tunic. She had the unsettling feeling that she'd caught him half-naked, so much of him seemed to be revealed as he sat playing his harmonica with his back to her. He controlled his breath brilliantly, throwing in little arpeggios, playing around with the melodies. He slid into "Oh, What A Beautiful Morning," from a new Broadway musical, and then "I Went to Kansas City."

"Do 'Surrey With the Fringe On Top,'" she urged, forgetting for the moment that he didn't know she was there.

Freddy wheeled around angrily, but Ruth had taken off her eyeglasses and put them in front of her on the counter. She couldn't see him very well. She leaned dreamily against the counter smiling at him. Freddy softened. He'd never seen Ruth's eyes shining. "Hi. I haven't got it right yet," he said. "Sing a few bars. Maybe I can get it."

"Ducks and Geese and Chicks better scurry...." Her voice was gritty, but she could sing on key. Freddy joined in with his harmonica, and she corrected him a few times, as if he were in the Elementary School Band; then they tried it again from the beginning, and they tried "Don't Throw Bouquets at Me," carefully picking their way through the melody from memory, not sure where it would go next, humming some of the words they didn't know, but when they got to the last line, "People will say we're in love," Ruth broke off suddenly (that pronoun "we" again.) Freddy stopped mid-note. The store went suddenly quiet, too quiet. Ruth felt out of breath. She struggled to say something, but the words of the song were playing around in her head, confusing her. Freddy was still four stools away from her at the counter, but, looking at her like that, he seemed so close she might suffocate. She fumbled along the counter for her glasses, unable to take her eyes off Freddy.

"I'm sorry," she managed as the silence stretched out. "I snuck up on you. I didn't mean.... The music.... I just stopped by for some aspirin."

"Headache?"

"Long day, I guess. Do you know that kid Tommy Randolph?"

Ruth looked so young without her glasses on. Freddy wanted to keep her talking. "Plays the trumpet," he said, nearly whispering, not wanting to loosen the tension he felt between them. "Mom's pretty well used up. Lives with that old Filipino out back?"

"Marian feeds him." Ruth peered up at him nearsightedly, blinking. He'd never seen her without her glasses. Her eyes, he realized, were pale, nearly turquoise blue, with a glint to them. She had thick eyelashes that kind of curled up at the ends. He wanted to look at her eyes more closely. Maybe even touch her cheek. What was he thinking? He was a married man. He always thought of himself as a married man. He still wore his wedding ring, even though Molly had been dead for six years. Ruth was the school principal for crying out loud. What was he thinking?

He was thinking that she was adorable.

Freddy had no idea what he was saying. He would have said anything to keep Ruth next to him. "Yeah, Marian takes him to the doctor, too," he said.

"And I suppose you give him his medicine for free," she said, gazing at him.

"Well, you know, I get all these samples." ("Stay here with me," he begged silently while he struggled to come up with something to say out loud.) "You want some aspirin?" he asked finally.

Ruth laughed. He'd broken the spell.

"No," she said, "I've changed my mind. Play me one more tune, and I'll go home."

Freddy could hardly make his lips work. He played another chorus of "Oh, What a Beautiful Morning," but it was sloppy. Ruth put her glasses back on. Tongue-tied, Freddy watched her leave. He didn't even say goodbye.

Freddy found himself abandoned in the darkened store. The ceiling creaked as the wind blew up the river from San Francisco Bay. It blew through a building too empty, too quiet. Freddy felt as if his life lay flapping in the evening breeze, closed down, vacant, uninhabited.

He was irritated with himself. Why hadn't he been able to invent an excuse to keep Ruth there -- one more song, another topic of conversation. Why hadn't he been quick enough to come up with a suggestion to meet her next week somewhere for dinner, Sacramento, maybe, a movie. She'd snuck up on him. He was out of practice. Six years....

What was he thinking? Lionel was at home waiting for his dinner while his father indulged in lonely fantasies in an empty store. No wonder the kid had problems.

Ike was waiting for Freddy the next morning.

"So, Fred, what were you and Ruth Hardy doing in the Drug Store last night?" Ike was busy with an order of eggs, over easy. His back was to the counter. He didn't see Freddy blush crimson.

"Came in for aspirin. Had some trouble with that Randolph kid, I guess." Freddy tried his best to sound off-hand.

Dan Martin came to his rescue, "Yeah, I heard Shirley Randolph put on quite a show at Joe's yesterday."

"I heard there was some harmonica playing," Ike said, pouring some pancakes on the griddle -- yeast raised, smelling like beer.

"What?" asked Harvey Lemmon. "Where?" Everybody at the counter was listening now.

"And some singing. Two-part harmony's what I heard." Ike eased two eggs on to a plate, slipped a stack of buttered toast on beside them. Never even turned around. Freddy could have killed him.

"We got a romance on our hands?" Harvey asked.

"Christ. Ruth came in for an aspirin as I was closing up, caught me practicing, said I was playing it wrong, corrected me. Period." He picked up the Sports Section.

"That sounds like her," said Bill Pratt.

"Freddy's too smart to get tangled up with that woman," Gino Ferrera said. "She'd eat him alive."

"And spit out the pieces," said Joe Scoleri laughing.

"And poor Lionel'd have to pack up and get out of town," Harvey said.

They all liked Freddy, felt kind of protective about him.

Ike flipped his pancakes. Freddy concentrated on the ball scores.

Ruth was on the phone to the District Office trying to explain why she hadn't filed some report she'd never heard of and probably lost. The songs from "Oklahoma" kept playing around in her head. Her blotter was covered with doodles.

"Say, that's shaping up to be quite an election down your way," Superintendent Graham said.

"Is it?" Ruth didn't pay much attention to local politics except when there was a school bond on the ballot. To be honest, Ruth was having trouble paying attention this morning, period.

"They say this young lawyer running against Jack Sullivan is putting up quite a race for Board of Supervisors. And he's a Ferrera. Got more relations than you can shake a stick at. Sullivan's running scared, is what I hear."

"That a fact." Ruth was interested now.

"Sullivan doesn't think he's got the votes to get re-elected."

"Is Sullivan a pretty good guy?" Ruth asked.

"I think so. He's always been pretty good on schools."

"I wonder what he'd do for 200 votes."

"Probably murder his own mother. Why?"

"Oh, nothing. I was thinking of maybe doing a little voter registration in Japan Town."

This time when Ruth dropped by Tosh's shoe repair shop, she had 200 voter registration forms she'd gotten from Elsie at the Post Office, "How many new citizens did you turn out in your citizenship class, Tosh?"

"Everybody passed except old Mrs. Adachi."

"Fifty? A hundred?"

"Maybe more. I ran three classes, actually."

"Are any of them registered to vote?"

"Not yet. I've got to get on that. There's an election coming up."

"Well, I've been doing some thinking...."

When she outlined her plan to Tosh, he was skeptical.

"Would Sullivan believe us?"

"What have we got to lose?" asked Ruth.

"Our houses," said Tosh.

"You'll lose those anyway. You can't afford these new rents."

"I don't know Miss Hardy...."

But a week later Tosh Nakamura, Ruth Hardy and the Reverend Miyasaki from the Buddhist Temple drove up the River Road to Sacramento to keep their appointment with Supervisor Sullivan. Tosh had 187 signatures of newly registered voters in his jacket pocket, each signature drawn in perfect cursive script ("Over the mountain; into the valley.") It seemed to Ruth that Tosh was sitting up straighter. The Reverend Miyasaki sat beside Ruth in the front seat, his back straight, his palms pressed flat down on the lap of his robe, his eyes staring straight ahead, as if he were meditating on their strange errand. But the silent, dignified presence of a Buddhist priest in his gray robes lent solemnity to their petition. It flustered the receptionists and impressed the Supervisor. There was no doubt in anybody's mind that they could deliver the votes they said they could deliver.

Ten days before the election, two county building inspectors appeared in Two Sloughs. They spent the morning in Japan Town, then called on Mr. Bream in his apartment above the bank. The next day it was Mr. Bream himself who stuck his head out the window upstairs, above the preposterous pillars on the Bank of Thurgood Bream.

"You, Missy." Mr. Bream pointed his fly swatter at Ruth, "You had something to do with this."

"Good morning," Ruth called up.

"I don't know how, but this is your doing," Mr. Bream yelled down at her. Everybody on the street looked up.

"One man; one vote," called out Ruth. "It's in the seventh grade civics book."

"You've bitten off more than you can chew this time, Missy. You've got $293 in the bank, and that's a fact. Pray you never need a loan, Miss Principal."

Immediately a second head appeared at the window. Ruth waived and ducked into her car. She winced. She didn't relish having the Breams as enemies. She probably would hear her bank balance shouted out the window from this day forward. The next day she left a jar of Royal Blenheim apricot jam made from her mother's recipe at the feet of the monster clock. Should the school principal stoop to such tactics? Was it a pitiful gesture? Yes, but it was darned good apricot jam, take it or leave it.

Even so, the Japanese community outdid her. A week later Tosh Nakamura appeared at the Bream's door with two packages. One contained a pair of deep purple velveteen pants and a pullover, hand stitched with elasticized waists, wrists and ankles, the perfect outfit for yoga. The other package contained two inlaid bamboo-handled fly swatters hand carved by Takao Ogawa, who made the finest fishing rods in the county. Tosh bowed politely to Mr. Bream and said that the Japanese community would like to thank him for his generosity in reducing their rents. He said the women of the community would like to take turns cleaning his apartment once a week to show their special appreciation. And from that day on, the greasy black mahogany furniture took on a special luster, and the ashtray on the dining table was emptied once a week. Ruth never saw it, of course. She was declared unwelcome every time Thurgood Bream spied her out his upstairs window.

November

Mrs. Weaver appeared at Ruth's office door one afternoon in early November. At first Ruth didn't recognize her. She'd only seen her once before, and that had been behind the shotgun her husband had been pointing at Ruth's head, while he told her to get out and stay out and leave his kids alone, just before he shot her tire to smithereens. But that had been two years ago. The kids had showed up every year since then, for a couple of months in the fall, then sometimes again in the spring. They were good kids, three girls and a boy. Rita, the middle girl, was smart, a whiz at math.

"Mrs. Weaver, come in. Sorry about the mess." Ruth moved a pile of achievement tests off a chair and offered it to Mrs. Weaver.

"I won't take much of your time, Miss Hardy." She remained standing at the door of Ruth's office, with both hands in front of her, kneading the handle of her handbag, staring over Ruth's left shoulder until Ruth had the urge to turn and see if there was something there. Ruth didn't try to make small talk. She could see this was hard enough for the woman standing before her. She sat down at her desk and waited.

"You see, I need work," Mrs. Weaver said finally.

"I see," said Ruth, not really seeing at all.

"Oh, I been workin'," Mrs. Weaver rushed to reassure her. "Two shifts. Afternoon and nights at the packing shed. That way I kin git'em off in the mornin'. Sue's old enough to git supper."

"She's a good girl," Ruth said, "they all are."

Mrs. Weaver looked at her then, for the first time. Her eyes glinted with pride and fear. Two shifts, Dear God! Tired eyes, but they were the color of steel.

"We gotta stay the winter, Miss Hardy. They cain't be battin' around different schools like they has been. And the packing shed's shut down for the season."

"Does your husband have work?" Ruth asked, remembering that clenched face and that shotgun.

"Some...." Mrs. Weaver was looking wall-eyed again. "He's... see... he's sick a lot. But I kin work," she glared at Ruth this time, and strong bones showed beneath her weather-beaten cheeks, "I kin do anything -- take in washing, scrub floors, prune. This house we got don't cost much. It's only to hold us over 'til asparagus season."

"I'd like to have the kids all year, Mrs. Weaver. That Suzanne is the best saxophone player I've got. And your Rita has a knack for arithmetic. I'll ask around."

Mrs. Weaver turned, "I won't keep you then. They know how to work," she said half way out the door, "Don't let 'em git away with nothin'."

Ruth watched her slip out the door. She had dressed up, Ruth thought. She wore cotton stockings, rolled at the knees and her good brown pumps. Her dress was clean and mended. The white crocheted collar was pressed. Two shifts. Three to eleven, eleven to seven. Her husband probably didn't know she had come. She had all her hopes pinned on those girls. And on Ruth. What chance did they have? If they didn't die of pneumonia out there. That place didn't have heat. Heck, it didn't have window glass in half the windows. Once the tule fog settled in.... She made a mental note to keep those kids after school as much as she could this winter on some pretext or another. And they'd need coats. Maybe Ike could use a dishwasher.

Ike had a better idea. He'd watched Bill Pratt every morning. All the men had. Ike tried to urge an extra egg into him, a pancake or two. But Bill was too tired to eat. He just sat nursing his coffee, growing thinner and thinner. The men didn't ask. They squeezed his shoulder as he sat hunched at the counter, asked if he needed help on his front gate. (Somebody'd noticed him out front working on it.) They kept an eye on him, the way they would keep an eye on a pump that seemed to be about to give out. They layed off the subject of Mavis. Mavis was dying.

"The nights are the toughest," Bill offered one morning.

"You getting any sleep at all?" Dan Martin asked.

Bill shrugged.

The men took note of the shrug, mulled it over.

"Say, Ruth sent a woman by," Ike said to nobody in particular, "wife of the guy who took a potshot at her out on Andrus Island that time. This woman needs work bad, any kind of work. Days...." He paused. "Nights. I could hire her for a couple hours in the afternoon, but I don't need her. Anybody could use any help?"

Ike made the rounds with the coffeepot. When he stopped in front of Bill Pratt he said, "I like the look of her. She's a worker. Hands like washboards."

Bill looked up, hollow-eyed, "Nights?" he asked

"She'd work nights."

"It isn't pretty."

"She's tough, Bill. I got a feeling she's seen it all."

Mavis Pratt died in late November. It took the town by surprise. She'd been dying for months. But dead is different. Bill Pratt wilted, as if root rot had set in. His friends clasped his arm, shook his hand, trying somehow to prop him up. Then they shuffled off, discouraged.

All except Freddy. Freddy stayed. He remembered how it felt to be adrift in sorrow, blind to the people rushing around you, deaf to their clumsy condolences, day and night running together. Freddy remembered it all. So he left Josephine Lemmon in charge of the Pharmacy for the week and told her he'd drop by at two every afternoon to fill prescriptions. Then he set himself up at Bill Pratt's kitchen table while Mrs. Weaver quietly worked around him. She was so careful to stay out of the way that Bill seldom saw her, and Freddy forgot that she was there. She made no attempt at conversation. She had been there at the end. There was nothing more to be said. While the men ate a bite of lunch in the kitchen, Mrs. Weaver did up the bedroom. While they listened to the radio in the living room, she cleaned the kitchen. Freddy doubted that anyone had actually hired her. She just kept coming after Mavis died.

Freddy answered the telephone, fended off the kindly callers, accepted the macaroni and cheese casseroles, rehashed and rehashed Mavis's final hours. No, there was nothing more Bill could have done. Yes, it had been time. She was ready to go. He gently put off Bill's children who wanted to "take Dad's mind off Mom," and clean out Mavis's closet and drawers, "get everything settled for Dad," organize the funeral. Freddy watched Bill battle the fatigue and the nightmare vision of Mavis at the end, pinched, waxy, eaten away by pain, and the resentment growing under his skin toward Mavis for leaving him alone like this, numb with exhaustion and grief, ill-equipped for life alone. Freddy didn't talk much to Bill. He didn't need to.

"I can't describe it," Bill said one evening, staring straight ahead, talking to nobody in particular. Freddy knew what he meant.

When Freddy got home at night he was haunted by his own memories. Molly's death and Mavis's death became confused in his own mind. He seemed to be revisiting that awful, gray time. He thought angrily of Molly. He couldn't even remember her face. He had snapshots, of course, but he couldn't actually see her face. How could Molly have been so careless as to drive off the levee and get herself killed?

But it was just that wild, carefree spirit that had fatally attracted him. He couldn't remember her face. He could remember her red hair, streaked with gold by the sun, and the freckled skin on her arms and her shoulders that turned gold, too, in summer. But her small rounded breasts were always white, and her belly was white, so that her deep red pubic hair surprised him with its darker color, its lushness, its curliness. He remembered kissing it, curling it on his forefinger, playing with those deep red curling strands....

Molly still haunted him, silently. He couldn't see her face though, alive, close to his, the way he had seen Ruth's face. How had Ruth gotten mixed up in this sad business? His mind was playing tricks on him. Molly haunted him silently. Ruth wafted in on a melody, her moist lips curved around an open note. Now when he played his harmonica he saw Ruth's face. And that scared the hell out of him.

"Men are terrible at death," Charlene groused to Ruth as they lugged the funeral flower arrangements to Charlene's car.

Mavis had specified that Charlene shouldn't have to do the flowers for her funeral. "She knew you'd be too broken up, dear," was how Retta Mae put it.

"What the hell," Charlene had grumped. "I've already bought up every yellow hothouse rosebud in Sacramento." Charlene was the town florist. She knew it, and so did everybody else. In a town the size of Two Sloughs, that meant somebody drove to Sacramento and bought flowers from the wholesale florist, brought them home and fixed them in her garage. That was Charlene. And she was no slouch either. She was "artistic." She could do bridesmaids' bouquets, Buddhist funeral arrangements, Rotarian banquets, you name it.... She threw in weeds and cattails and pieces of people's hedges. Her husband Larry nearly killed her one time when he found her out in the orchard cutting sprigs of pear blossoms for some wedding bouquet. But she could make a carnation look like it had been alive at one time or another. Not every small-town florist could.

"I'm not coping well," Charlene said as Ruth helped her load the funeral arrangements into the back seat of her car. "When Retta Mae goes into her 'do good' mode, it always brings out the worst in me."

"The flowers are gorgeous," Ruth said.

"For a funeral that was so damned well organized, she picked a rotten month for flowers. Nothing but chrysanthemums."

Mavis's funeral went off without a hitch. She had specified yellow roses. She had chosen the pallbearers. She had picked out the songs for the choir: "Nearer My God to Thee" and a hymn that sounded like "Love, Oh Love, Oh Careless Love" but wasn't. Ruth sang alto. There were always enough sopranos.

Mavis had requested that Pastor Rehmke come out of retirement to perform the service. Ruth thought his slow mournful tone, the result of a stroke, suited the occasion. Bill Pratt sat in the front pew, bolstered by his brother and Freddy on one side and his children on the other. People said that Freddy was taking Mavis's death almost as hard as Bill was. Ruth worried about Charlene. Then the new Presbyterian minister, whom Mavis had sought to avoid, chimed in, talking the way young ministers did, like a politician, sailing up at the end of every sentence. He broke the spell. By the time he asked people to stand up and share their memories of Mavis, the mood of the crowd had shifted dangerously. It had turned surly. Nobody opened his mouth, figuring it was none of this politico-preacher's damned business what they remembered about Mavis. The entire population of Two Sloughs sat with heads bowed and waited the guy out. Finally the choir sang "Rock of Ages," which Mavis had requested, at too slow a tempo, in Ruth's opinion, Old Pastor Rehmke blessed them, though they knew they didn't deserve it, and they all filed out.

Refreshments were served at Retta Mae's house out on Dead Horse Island. Everybody went. Retta Mae organized the whole thing according to Mavis's posthumous plan: devilled eggs, jello ring molds, carrot salad, date bars, and, of course, Ruth's finger size chicken sandwiches. It was muddy out at Retta Mae's. Charlene drove with Ruth because Larry had gone out early to help park cars. Even so, they had to park in the alfalfa field behind the house, not sure they could back out again. It began to drizzle.

They wore their least sensible shoes, in honor of Mavis. Ruth balanced her mounded platter of eight dozen finger-sized chicken sandwiches. Charlene carried an enormous flower arrangement, "just the leftovers," she said, rosebuds, daisies and some hothouse lilies that must have cost Charlene a fortune this time of year. They teetered across the alfalfa field toward the house, their high heels sinking into the mud. Charlene's mascara had smeared.

"One of the troubles is I've got cancer myself," said Charlene glumly.

"Charlene..."

"I found out last summer. Didn't tell Mavis. Didn't want to horn in. Didn't want to depress her. Then it got too late to tell her.... Anyway Doc thinks they took care of it. All through the service, I kept thinking, Jesus, Mavis, how are the rest of us going to top this?"

"Charlene...." Ruth was thinking fast, but her wheels were spinning.

Suddenly, out of the drainage ditch to their left came a whole flock of Canadian geese. Retta Mae had befriended a pair in the fall, and they had taken up more or less permanent residence at her place. Retta Mae fed them bread crusts and chick scratch. But apparently they had company, because six or seven geese headed for them, coming on fast with their necks stretched low and long, looking for trouble. Charlene, balancing her bouquet, shooed them with her free hand. Ruth shooed with another, but a finger sandwich slipped as she waved, and those geese were on it before it hit the ground. Ruth fought off the geese, but they had spotted the rest of the sandwiches under the tea towel. Charlene shouted and kicked geese, which isn't easy in high heels in the mud in the rain. She kicked her feet right out from under her straight skirt and slid down with the flower arrangement on top of her.

Ruth didn't know Canadian geese liked rosebuds. Or maybe they thought they were something else, fat grubs or giant salmon eggs. By the time Ruth hauled Charlene out from under those geese, eight dozen finger sandwiches lay strewn all over the alfalfa field. If Harvey Lemmon hadn't come along with a shotgun on the gun rack of his pickup and fired his twelve gauge into the air a couple of times, they might never have gotten out of that alfalfa field. By the time they got back on their feet they were smeared head to toe with mud and mayonnaise and green alfalfa. Harvey and Larry wiped them both off as best they could, considering they were, all four of them, falling over laughing.

"I'm liking this better all the time," said Charlene. "It's getting messier."

"Yeah," Ruth said, "you don't want a funeral to be too well organized." But Ruth felt suddenly bereft. Charlene was her only real friend in town, the only person who didn't see her as a school principal first and a woman second, the only person who would tell her the dress she was wearing was frumpy or that her hair looked better that way. Charlene had a "painterly eye," or what Ruth took to be one. Her vision of the world was skewed so that she often missed the main point but delighted Ruth with her keen observation of the telling details, her offbeat captions. "Charleneisms" had become a staple in the lore of Two Sloughs. It was Charlene who lovingly called Ike "Over Easy," for his round bald head. It was Charlene who referred to the local crop duster as "Fly By Night" for his amorous escapades in Two Sloughs. Ruth felt a lump in her own gut, as if Charlene's revelation had lodged there. She didn't like the idea of Charlene and funerals in the same sentence.

Ruth hadn't seen Freddy since the funeral. She had half expected him to call, but since Mavis's death he had devoted himself to Bill Pratt. If Mavis was so well organized, why couldn't she have put off her death a few weeks, thought Ruth, just until Freddy had time to call? She felt ashamed of herself before she had even finished the thought. Mavis had suffered enough, God knows. Anyway, how long does it take to call? Freddy had had time to call. Maybe he seized upon Mavis's death as an excuse not to call. Charlene seemed to be avoiding Ruth, too. Was she sorry that she'd betrayed her cancer scare to Ruth? November is a bleak month on the river, thought Ruth, if you aren't a duck hunter.

Clarinet practice was always a nightmare. By November they were ready for everything; proficient at nothing. But John Philip Sousa brought out the worst in them, it seemed to Ruth. And high C? What was the man thinking of? They couldn't get through the first repeat of "Stars and Stripes Forever." Ruth beat the time out for them, "bum bum BUM; bum bum BUM; bum bum BUM..., " beat it out on their music stands with her baton, beat it out on their heads. "Crisp attack. Use your tongues. Blow, Sally! You're not making any sound at all, for crying out loud."

Barbara Kramer had fallen off her horse and broken her arm, leaving Ruth and the rest of the clarinet section without a strong first chair. Barbara was blonde and bossy, and wore fuzzy pink angora sweaters that drove the eighth grade boys wild, but she played in tune and she played loud. Without her all Ruth had was spit and squawks and an occasional breathy C. Sally Martin was hopeless, as far as Ruth could see. She hated the dry rasp of the reed against her tongue. Ruth could see her grimace every time she put the clarinet in her mouth. She had sat beside Barbara Kramer for three years faking it. None of the other girls showed any promise. None of them practiced at home. Their approach was to play softly enough so they didn't get into trouble. Seldom had Ruth heard so little noise come out of so many girls.

Ruth stomped back to her office to escape the reedy sounds and the fingernail-on-the-blackboard squeaks in the auditorium. She had told the clarinets to practice those ten measures until they got them right -- all night if necessary. Twelve heads had ducked as they chewed on their mouthpieces. Twelve sets of eyes had peered up at her over their music stands. Fumiko Matsubara was a merciless mimic. She was probably giving the girls an imitation of Miss Hardy's lecture right now.

Mr. Mundorf had brought the mail, and the notice of the State Band Competition had come. Ruth opened it anxiously. If Barbara Kramer's broken arm didn't heal, they were in trouble. They had moved the State Competition up to March 1 this year. That gave her even less time than usual. Her strategy was to plan the Two Sloughs Elementary School Music Festival two weeks before the State Band Competition. That gave her a good dress rehearsal for the State Competition and two weeks to iron out the worst problems. She had learned that the rainy season was the best time to rope fathers into making sets, and after Christmas and Chinese New Year was the best time to get mothers to help with costumes. March 1 was definitely pushing it. She scanned the entry form and the rules of the competition:

THIS YEAR BANDS WILL BE JUDGED ON THEIR UNIFORMS AS WELL AS THEIR MUSIC.

Uniforms! Ruth had had trouble in years past getting enough white shirts together to present a fairly unified front. Uniforms! What the heck was the State thinking of? Were they judging bands on the amount of money each School District had? Ruth reached for the telephone. But the District Superintendent was in a meeting, which, in Ruth's opinion, was where the District Superintendent always was.

"Well, when he gets out, tell him I'm mad. No, tell him I'm furious. Tell him to get busy and go to bat for us. No, tell him to call Ruth Hardy at Two Sloughs Elementary. We have a crisis on our hands." She was surprised when Nettie Crane from the phone company didn't come on the line to find out what the crisis was.

The District Superintendent called back moments later, and he seemed mildly irritated by the "crisis." "But, Ruth," he said, "some schools go to a lot of trouble over their uniforms. They should get some credit for all that effort."

"We go to a lot of trouble getting shoes on the feet of our kids. Do we get any credit for that? Who's going to tell my kids they don't have a prayer of winning the Band Contest this year because they aren't rich enough? You or me?"

"Ruth, your band always does well. I'm sure you'll do well again this year."

"Horse manure. I don't want to do well. I want to win. You call those S.O.B.s and tell them that their rules are discriminatory. You tell them I'll take it up with the Attorney General's office if they give me any more hassle. Dan Martin's brother is in the Attorney Generals office, so I can do it. I've got the Board of Supervisors in my back pocket, too. You tell 'em that. You've got one week. I'll expect to hear from you by Tuesday." She slammed down the phone. "Sons of bitches," she said under her breath. She looked at the trophies in the case in her office. This was a big deal for this town. For six years in a row they had been finalists in the State Band Competition, competing with bands that were bigger, wealthier and had better instruments by far. She had to make do with lots of clarinets and trumpets because they were cheaper than tubas and French horns and trombones. She had only been able to scrape up enough to afford one used tuba and two dented trombones.

She was taking this too personally, she thought. This wasn't the Mozart Festival. She swiveled her chair, gazed out the window. She had gone to Salzburg on a summer exchange program in college, before the war, a summer of Mozart and *lieder* and *knockerln* and *obst torte.* The high summer pastures filled with buttercups, wild roses along the road, embroidered costumes, glorious music -- Ruth had never gotten over it. She still had her dirndl hanging in the back of her closet. She would push for a summer-long round of concerts and recitals in Two Sloughs if it weren't for pear season and the fact that she had enough on her hands getting the Two Sloughs Elementary School Chorus and Band into shape for one two hour performance.

She had to laugh at herself. Who was she kidding? She never should have entered the State Band Competition in the first place. Her ambition had gotten the better of her. They were in the category of schools with 500 pupils or less. They could also have qualified for schools of 250 pupils or less, but no such category existed. The band had to have at least 40 members. By repairing some of those old trumpets and adding a few ringers in the percussion section, she had always been able to scrape up a band of 40. But uniforms! She couldn't possibly justify the expense of uniforms for kids who didn't even have winter coats.

She knew she got carried away with her Music Festival, that the town grumbled about it, didn't think it was necessary to make such a production out of it, only indulged her because they saw how important it was to her. But darn it all, it was the only time in their lives some of these kids ever would be behind footlights. She wanted them to know what it felt like to work like heck, to be scared and then... feel that surge of adrenaline, that burst of applause. She wanted them to know that if they practiced hard enough, worked long enough, they could do anything they wanted to do, be anything they wanted to be. Why she had been Papagena, for crying out loud. She went back to her clarinets.

December

Maybe it was the fogged windows, but Ike's seemed to Ruth to be even clubbier in early December. The men didn't seem to be in a hurry to go anywhere. The full ashtrays and the empty mugs indicated they'd been sitting a while. It had started to rain finally, and it was coming down as if it meant business. They couldn't even prune in this weather. The talk had turned to duck hunting. The men seemed glad to see Ruth walk in the door, just for the diversion.

"Lucky you didn't drown out there, Ruth," Ike said, sliding a mug of coffee across the counter to her.

"Nearly did. Thanks, Ike."

Ruth sat at the near end of the counter, cradling the mug of coffee in both hands as she listened to the chatter. Freddy, she noticed, sat at the far end.

"They say it's not going to let up either."

"I don't relish another Christmas flood."

"Never happen. These storms are too cold."

"Snowing down to 2000 feet, is what I heard."

"Speaking of cold," Ruth said after a minute or two, "I got some migrant kids, don't have coats."

"Migrants? What are they doin' still here?"

"It's that Weaver family out back on Andrus Island. They're staying the winter out there."

"Isn't that the gang ran you off with a shotgun?"

Ruth grinned, "Yeah, well..."

"Now they're holding you up for coats?" Harvey Lemmon teased her.

"Call it 'protection.' I'm buying myself a little protection," Ruth said. "Say, the woman's a worker. She says you might be hiring her to do a little dish washing, Ike."

Ike looked up and sighed. "So that's it," he said.

Ruth knew she only came in here when she wanted something. It embarrassed her to always have her hand out some way. The fact that the town was generous didn't make it any less embarrassing. She felt like the Salvation Army, as though she should have a tambourine, for heck's sake. She noticed that Freddy was watching her from the far end of the counter.

"Actually, that's not all," Ruth said uncomfortably, mentally rattling her tambourine. "Say, could I get a doughnut -- cake with powdered sugar?"

The men at the counter all watched Ike slide a cake doughnut, with powdered sugar, onto a plate and put it in front of her. She could feel a hint of anticipation in the air. But they were all duck hunters. They knew how to sit and wait. "Ruth, coming in at 3:00 o'clock," is how they would have put it to themselves.

Ruth took a bite. Delicious. "The thing is," she said, then took a sip of her coffee, tried again. "It's this State Band Competition...."

"You're a cinch to win it this year," Dan Martin said. "With that Randolph kid at first trumpet...".

"You'd a won last year if the judges hadn't been taken in by the fancy hats and all that gold braid on that band from Lafayette," Harvey Lemmon said.

"That's just it, Harvey," Ruth said disgustedly. "The fancy hats and the gold braid. They count this year. Legally. We're judged on uniforms this year. Two Sloughs doesn't have a chance."

"They can't do that," Ike said.

Ruth took a big bite of her doughnut, just to dry her mouth out.

"Well they have," she said with her mouth full so that she sounded sort of choked up.

"Then we'll damn well have to get uniforms," Dan said.

"Heck," said Ruth miserably, "I'm still working on winter coats. I can't justify spending money on band uniforms."

"We won't spend money. We'll make them." Freddy said.

"This isn't some gypsy operetta, Freddy, like we do for the Music Festival, where we round up everybody's old bridesmaid dresses and cut 'em off to fit sixth graders. This State Competition is over our heads. I'm going to have to pull out."

"And tell the kids you're quitting? That you're not even going to try?" Freddy asked.

"I'm not going to make them the laughing stock of the Competition," Ruth said angrily, knowing that it was she who didn't want to be humiliated up in Sacramento. She was sorry now that she had even brought the subject up. "You always said it was too much trouble anyway," she said nastily.

"It is too much trouble," Freddy said hotly. "That's no reason not to do it."

In the uncomfortable silence that followed, Ruth dug in her raincoat pocket, put a quarter on the counter. Freddy had a lot of nerve lecturing to her about trying. She was breaking her neck over their darned kids. Freddy, who didn't even trouble to keep his one lousy kid in line. "Thanks, Ike," she said hoarsely. "I'd better be going."

"What did you have to make her mad for, Freddy?" Harvey asked.

"What did she have to go and give up for?" Freddy shot back. "She's the one who pounded into those kids that they could do anything if they wanted it bad enough."

"She's right, though. It doesn't make any sense to spend money on band uniforms," Harvey said. "It's crazy."

"That's never stopped her before," Ike said. "I'm going to run this by Emma tonight. See what she thinks."

Ruth left Ike's furious at Freddy, hurt. The bottom of her stomach felt as if somebody'd dug a hole in it and then gone off without planting anything. The rest of her seemed in danger of caving into it. How could Freddy speak to her like that, from the farthest end of Ike's counter, as if he were trying to put distance between them? How could he sound so angry?

How could she let Freddy get under her skin? He was such an impractical man that it irritated her. If he had any sense of school budgets.... If he'd ever served on the School Board like some of the other more responsible men, he'd never have made such an idiotic statement. If anybody squeezed more out of a school budget than she did.... How dare he accuse her of quitting? How could he talk to her like that after.... After what? She sighed. After she'd snuck up on him in his own store, and he'd tried to sell her aspirin?

Nevertheless, she didn't mention the State Competition at band practice that afternoon. They were tackling "The Star Spangled Banner," and she simply didn't feel up to dealing with the clarinets and the rockets' red glare and the State Band Competition all in one breath.

Janet Martin and Caroline Graham met at Ping Lowe's Grocery the next morning. They leaned against the meat counter, idly scuffing the sawdust on the floor. Charlene Jepsen joined in the discussion, while Ping himself offered suggestions from behind the counter as he trimmed the fat from a piece of beef round. The conversation centered on uniforms for the Two Sloughs School Band. Charlene's idea was to have a fund-raiser of some kind, a pot luck supper or something.

"It would have to be after Christmas," Janet warned.

"Better," Ping said. "after your New Year. Before Chinese New Year. I make pork rolls. I better talk to Lum Yee."

"From the whorehouse?" Caroline was shocked. "What could he do? How much money do we need? How much do uniforms cost?" she asked.

"I don't know. We need a chairman," said Janet. "How about Freddy Noble? I hear he's all in favor of band uniforms."

"I hear Fred and Ruth aren't speaking," Charlene said.

"If it's going to be in January, it could be a Tule Fog Party," Caroline suggested, "to celebrate the bleakest month of the year in Two Sloughs."

"Great Idea. Freddy'd be perfect," Charlene said. "We'll serve a Tule Fog punch, kind of green and misty, spiked with rum or something. What do you think, Ping?"

"O.K.," said Ping. "I make punch." Ping Lowe worked meticulously with his butcher's knife, trimming the round, cutting it into cubes for the grinder. Ping had lived in Two Sloughs all his life, except for the four years when he attended the University of California in Berkeley. Then his father had left a cousin in charge of the Grocery and opened a chop suey joint in Oakland so that Ping would have someplace to live -- a crowded flat above the restaurant -- and someplace to eat. Ping had earned his degree in mathematics, but his real passion was political science. Ping understood how Two Sloughs worked. The town was run by a triumvirate: Miss Hardy, Doc and Old Man Bream. Generally Miss Hardy and Doc were pitted against Bream, but not always.

Ping ground hamburger onto a square of heavy pink butcher paper, weighed it on his scale, then subtracted a handful of ground meat from the mound on his scale -- two pounds exactly. He added a little. This was the way it worked: politically, Miss Hardy had all the parents in her corner, past and present. Doc got all the young mothers because they ended up in his office exhausted and broke and desperate for comfort at a time when their husbands were too busy and too worried to bother with them. Doc got the men later, about forty, when they began to realize that they weren't going to be able to work eighty hours a week forever and that some of their dreams were going to stay dreams and that some of their fears were real. Old Man Bream owned the bank and the mortgages on all the farms. He had everybody on a short lead.

Ping went into the walk-in for more round steak. He knew that his family's existence in Two Sloughs was as precarious as the levees his grandfather helped build. His family lived in the cracks of the white world, scrabbling up along the edges of the town to buy a grocery store nobody else had the money to buy, or loan money when Old Man Bream wouldn't. They dug their roots into crevices in the town's smooth surface. Ping knew who was in debt, who couldn't pay his bills, who wasn't living at home much, who was drinking a lot. But he also knew that he had to watch his step. He knew what World War II was all about. Slant eye. Chink. Ping knew that a lot of racial hatred had started as nothing more than owing too much money to a Chinaman. Ping knew he had to be useful without ever becoming powerful. He wasn't shifty. He was careful. He went back to grinding the women's hamburger while the women chatted about their party, who would give it, who would tackle Freddy. What was going on between Freddy and Ruth anyhow? Somebody had to approach Ruth about the party. Maybe after Christmas. Let things settle a little bit. Ping kept his head down. Janet Martin was a stickler about too much fat in her ground round.

December gave Ruth and the teachers a break and put the pressure on the parents of Two Sloughs. For Ping Lowe it was an especially trying time. The grocery business turned frantic. The housewives of Two Sloughs grew hysterical as the count for their Christmas dinners rose and shrank. Orders for turkeys and standing rib roasts had to be kept track of. The shelves had to be stocked constantly. The wholesale warehouses shorted the little stores on cranberry sauce and canned yams.

When Ping finally got home to China Camp at night, his daughter Cheryl nagged him to string Christmas tree lights or to mail letters to Santa Claus. Most of the year Ping and his wife didn't pay much attention to the religious mix in Two Sloughs. Cheryl often went home from school on Tuesdays with Susie Scoleri because the nuns gave both girls Tootsie Pops if they showed up at catechism (and because the cement walks that ran around the Catholic church were wide and smooth and the best place in town to roller skate.)

But Christmas wasn't really a Buddhist holiday.

"Why not?" Cheryl demanded one night.

"Because we're Buddhists. We don't believe that Jesus was the son of God."

"Then what about the Apostles' Creed?" demanded Cheryl and then horrified Ping by reciting the Apostles' Creed, word for word.

"She also know twenty riddle 'What black and white and red all over?'" said his wife. "Also jump rope rhyme. Also opening to radio program --

'Return with us now....thrilling days of yesteryear.' You ask her. Forty-eight states and capitols. She know it all."

Ping groaned and unlaced his shoes. "Reverend Chow have a stroke, she tell him Apostles' Creed," he said.

"One minute you want Cheryl be American," said his wife. "Next you want Chinese. What you want?"

Ping sighed. He was exhausted. His feet hurt. "No Christmas light," he said. "No tree. Nobody in China Camp caught dead with Christmas tree." But he told his wife Cheryl could have one present, new roller skates. His wife also bought her a new red sweater and mittens to wear to the Living Nativity at the Catholic Church. It was always freezing cold at the Living Nativity.

"No worry," his wife reassured him. "We Chinese, we got firecrackers. Every kid in town is Chinese for Chinese New Year."

Ruth had planned to spend Christmas at her sister Jeanie's in Oregon. It was a good time to get away. School was out. People around town were nice about inviting Ruth to Christmas dinner, but it was a family time. The town turned inward. Also it was raining.

A week before Christmas Jeanie called to say that two of the children had the stomach flu and Jeanie's husband had been laid off again. Jeanie thought it wasn't a good time.

"Are you sure you'll be all right by yourself?" Jeanie asked.

Ruth laughed, "are you sure you'll be all right?"

"Where can it go from here?" Jeanie said. "Oh Lord, got to go. Stuart's throwing up."

It was a relief in a way. Ruth thought guiltily of her sister. Ruth ought to be up there stuffing turkeys and wrapping packages. It wasn't a good time, Jeanie had said. Poor Jeanie. It was never a good time.

It rained all Christmas vacation. The river rose, turned the sullen color of diesel fuel. To Ruth, the river seemed ominously quiet. It ran thick with the mud of a thousand angry sloughs and ditches, fast with the flow of foothill creeks crashing out of the Sierra. But she could scarcely guess the brutal force of it unless she happened to glance out her car window to see a broken cottonwood tree sweep under the Two Sloughs Bridge, a whole tree flicked like a match stick under the roiling waters. Ruth had her own gauge of the river's height. She checked it every day against the spindly legs of Ike's Cafe. The river was high, but it had a good eight feet to go before it dampened the linoleum in Ike's Cafe. The legs were stained at the high water mark of four years ago. The water was still three feet below that. The sky was dark gray, the orchards were gray sticks wallowing in mud. Water stood in her flower beds; mallard and sprig floated in the flooded cornfields behind her house.

Ruth had already announced that she was going to be away for Christmas. She'd refused several invitations. None from Freddy. On Christmas Eve Ruth made herself a mug of hot chocolate, put two marshmallows in it and curled up in a chair by the fire listening to Handel's Messiah. She was determined not to feel sorry for herself. The hardest night of the year to be stubbornly independent had to be Christmas Eve. She turned the volume up on the Messiah and sat sipping her hot chocolate, letting the music pour over her. She didn't even hear the knocking on the door at first. She thought it was rain pounding on the roof.

"Ruth," It was Louie Riccetti, tapping on the window now, rain pouring off the brim of his duck hunting hat.

"Louie, sorry, I didn't hear you over the music. Come in. Merry Christmas." She was embarrassed to be caught in her bathrobe and slippers so early on Christmas Eve. It made her look abandoned. She was tempted to feign illness. No, she couldn't do that. Louie would call Doc and send him down to check on her.

But Louie didn't even notice her robe and slippers. "I can't come in, Ruth. I'm mud, up to my elbows. I brought you something. For helping me with the readin' and all. Here."

Louie pulled a shoe box out from under his slicker and thrust it into Ruth's arms. The box had holes in the top. "Her mother is the best little mouser we ever had around our place. She's a barn cat. She don't need much attention. She'll keep this place free of mice and rats, too."

"Louie, I..."

"No, don't open the box 'til you close the door. It'll take her a few days to get used to you. There's a can of food in there and a can of evaporated milk, to get her started. Well, the family's waiting. Merry Christmas, Ruth." And Louie ducked his head under the brim of his hunting hat and turned away, flustered by the tears forming in the corners of Ruth's eyes.

Ruth closed the door and went back to her chair by the fire. A Christmas present. Imagine Louie fixing up this little box, poking the holes in the top. She sat with the box in her lap contemplating it, waiting for her tears to dry up. Had Louie tied the ribbon too? It looked like it. The bow was pretty well worked over. The knot was good and tight.

A scratching sound came from inside the box. Oh Help! She was afraid of what she might find, but when she cautiously eased the cover off, what she found was more afraid than she was: a fuzzy calico ball with a black patch over one eye backed into the corner of the shoe box. The kitten hissed furiously at her, then shot out the side of the box. Ruth was too quick for her. She hadn't played second base all those years for nothing. She grabbed the kitten by the scruff of the neck as it leapt off her lap. The kitten shrieked, a high, ear-piercing yowl, and dug her claws into Ruth's thigh.

"Ow! Ruth yelped. Then she started to laugh. "Oh no, she said, "another darned Clarinet."

As she stroked the kitten, a scene from her childhood floated through her mind. Her father coming home from work and making the two girls guess which pocket -- an old game that Ruth usually won, being older and wiser in the ways of their father. But this time Jeannie spied a wiggle in his left pocket.

"From the Parts Department," he'd said winking, reaching into his pocket and with a magician's flourish, "Voila!" he'd produced a sleepy gray kitten snuggled in the palm of his hand.

Their mother had flatly refused to have a kitten. "Who's going to take care of it? Cat food... Hair all over the house.... How could you just...."

The girls had made elaborate promises. Had they kept them? And the kitten took up permanent residence on Jeannie's bed, which their mother said would lead to allergies.

Ruth and Clarinet sat listening to the Messiah in front of the fire all Christmas Eve. Ruth kept a firm grip on the tight little ball until finally she felt the kitten relax and begin to fall asleep in her lap, purring more or less in tune to the music.

January

After Christmas it was time to get into high gear on the Two Sloughs Music Festival. Ruth had sent in the entry for the State Band Competition because it didn't cost anything to enter, but she had pretty much dismissed the idea of going, unless they changed the rule about uniforms. She was still fighting mad about that. The State hadn't heard the last from her on that subject. At least the kids would have the local Music Festival. She had chosen a nautical theme this year because she had found four dozen white seaman's hats for a dollar a dozen at an Army Navy Surplus Store. She knew there were a few Navy uniforms around town. And God knows there were plenty of rowboats.

"Anchors Aweigh!" Never had she heard a more waterlogged version. She tapped her baton on her music stand. "Con Spirito," she said. "Con Spirito. What does that mean, people? Clarinets, there is not one note over high C in here. This should be easy for you. Clarinets alone, please, starting at measure 14. Sit up. One, two, three, four."

Mr. Mundorf poked his head in the auditorium as the clarinets ended their dirge. "We're ready to block out the sets. We bother you if we work up on the stage?"

"Just close the curtain. And keep your voices down."

The sixth grade boys trooped up onto the stage with their butcher paper sketches and their chalk, which caused a certain amount of tittering among the third clarinets, but by the end of the afternoon "Anchor Aweigh" seemed less destined for Davy Jones's locker.

Lionel Noble had switched from trumpet to trombone, and he seemed to be taking to it. It made Ruth nervous to put so much noise in the hands of so unreliable a band member, but it was the noise that seemed to intrigue Lionel. Ruth suspected he might be practicing on the sly. His tone began to sound remarkably round. Ronald Fujimoto and Tommy Randolph were good. The trumpet section had never sounded better. She'd like to tackle "Semper Fidelis" with those trumpets, but she wasn't sure she could ever crank the clarinets up to Allegro Marcato. On the other hand, a brisk staccato might be good for them. And Barbara Kramer was out of her arm cast.

After practice she climbed onto the stage to look at the sketches for the sets. Mr. Mundorf was an artist. His janitorial work was only an occupation for him. His real love was oil painting. He looked forward every year to helping the sixth graders design and paint the sets. He unrolled their butcher paper sketches now with a flourish. "This is going to be something," he said proudly. "This here'll knock 'em dead."

Oh, my God. A three masted square-rigger, with bowsprit, flying jib, topgallants and who knew what all. Ruth looked at Mr. Mundorf speechless with horror. Carl Mundorf was a gifted artist, but he wasn't much of an engineer. At last year's music festival "Tulip Time" Ruth had ended up with more fathers than third graders on the stage, battling to keep a refrigerator carton windmill upright. And every year Carl's ideas got grander. Carl had been going to too many movies.

"Of course it'll have to be cut down to scale," he reassured her. "I'm thinking 15 feet long, with 12 foot masts. It's hard to find bamboo longer than 12 feet."

"Now Carl, we don't want to get carried away. I was thinking more in terms of a row boat," Ruth said sternly.

"Oh, *ya*, well, you could use a row boat, too. Kind of like a dinghy. Tie it on to the back of the ship or something. She's a beauty, huh?"

Oh, boy. Ruth had visions of yards of sheeting falling down in the middle of the performance, bamboo masts drooping perilously during solos.

"I told the kids we'd make a paper-mache figurehead," Mr. Mundorf continued excitedly. "Lady Liberty. They want to call it the Stars and Stripes. Great, huh?"

"It's great. We don't have any money, though. I'm not sure we have enough...."

"We've got plenty. I mean to use up that dark blue exterior trim paint the County sent us by mistake. High gloss." Mr. Mundorf smacked his lips and rolled up his plans. "Yes sir, this'll knock their eyes out."

Ruth had to sit down. She felt limp. She found a chair in the wings and dragged it out onto the stage. She pretended to be studying Mr. Mundorf's sketches. Actually she was thinking about Mr. Mundorf.

Carl Mundorf had won a scholarship to study painting at the San Francisco Art Institute in 1916. The family must have pinned all their hopes on him. His mother Ada baked applesauce cakes for people around town, robust Germanic sheet cakes bulging with fat raisins and cocoa and chopped walnuts. Mr. Mundorf told Ruth that Ada had spent every penny of her applesauce cake money on a new overcoat and hat for him from the Sears and Roebuck catalogue. One September evening in 1916 Carl had stood on the stern of the grand old riverboat sweating in that stiff new overcoat and hat, clutching the suitcase his father had brought with him from Germany. He told Ruth it was the most wonderful day of his life. Ruth could almost see him waving until the paddle wheel swung around a bend in the river, then in the dusk, with the swallows swooping low along the water beside him, running forward to the bow, that young artist with such high hopes, holding his hat in his hand, letting the wind ruffle his hair, hoping to catch the first whiff of fog and the bohemian life that awaited him in San Francisco. It was her story of her summer in Austria, in reverse.

"Tell me what San Francisco was like in those days," Ruth said, "when you were a student down there."

Mr. Mundorf pushed his glasses up on his head and sighed. His good eye glazed over with memories. He was looking down at his drawings, but Ruth could see that he was seeing San Francisco, North Beach.

"It was a haven for artists in those days. We rented spare rooms and basements from those old Italian families who lived in North Beach. We drank the Dego red those old guys made in their garages, ate red spaghetti in their family-style restaurants -- all you could eat, with that sour, crusty bread. Wait here," he said.

He came back moments later with his dust mop and a dog-eared sketchbook full of fishermen's faces, old men playing bocce ball, beautiful work.

"Have you ever shown this to anyone, you know, a gallery or anything?" Ruth asked as she leafed through the book.

Mr. Mundorf leaned on the handle of his dust mop and laughed. "That's all over now," he said.

Ruth didn't press him. She knew the next chapter of the story. America entered the Great War against Carl's father's fatherland, and in 1918 Carl and his younger brother Jacob found themselves in Eastern France slogging through nettles and steep ravines in the thickest hardwood forest Carl said he ever hoped to see, wetter and colder that they had ever been in their lives. Carl had told her that the American troops were grass green and clumsy. The enemy looked like their cousins in Stockton, blonde and pink cheeked and scared. Rabbits ran through the woods zig zagging crazily. It never stopped raining, he said. Jacob died in a barnyard. Carl found him face down in a manure pile. Carl was hit by shrapnel nine days later and lost an eye, most of his cheek and his chance to return to the Art Institute. It was a great

American victory. It made General Pershing famous. Carl's father had a whole scrapbook of clippings about the Meuse-Argonne operation.

Carl returned to Two Sloughs to live with his heart-broken parents. He had told Ruth that his Sears and Roebuck overcoat still hung in the hall closet next to his army uniform. The pockets were filled with mothballs.

The Two Sloughs Music Festival was his one chance to indulge his passion for paint. At the bottom of the mimeographed program, Ruth always wrote, "sets created by Carl Mundorf, Artistic Director, and the sixth grade class." She watched him as he leaned over his sketches, shading in the keel, adding the figurehead. She held his yellowed sketchbook in her hand: an old man mending a fishing net in the sun, a crab pot delicately rendered....

She was in for it this year, and there wasn't a thing in the world she could do about it.

Ruth headed back to her office with visions of torn bed sheets and oil-based dark blue paint spinning crazily in her head. Sometimes these Two Sloughs Music Festivals got completely out of hand.

"There you are. I've been looking for you." Freddy Noble lugged a cardboard box down the hall. "I've got something to show you."

No apology. No hint that he had insulted her in front of everybody at Ike's, called her a quitter. Nothing. He simply shows up in the hallway a month later lugging a box. All excited. Why did this run-in remind her of her meeting with Mr. Mundorf? Freddy put the box down in the middle of the hallway, got down on his knees, rummaged in it, pulled a white jacket out and held it up.

Ruth, who was still recovering from three masted schooners and Mr. Mundorf's memories, stared blankly at him.

"The uniforms, Ruth! Forty of them! There's another box in your office."

"But those aren't...."

"Oh, I know, I know, they need gold braid, maybe some epaulets, but Shiz Ota and I have it all worked out. Lum Yee is getting the gold braid from some sweatshop he has a connection with in San Francisco. Shiz says they can turn these things into something that would make Annapolis graduates proud."

"Freddy, that's great, but we can't afford 40 jackets..."

"Don't have to, Ruth. See, they're pharmacists' tunics, size small. Pharmacists aren't wearing this heavy starched cotton any more. It's kind of an old fashioned style. They nearly gave them to me."

He's lying, Ruth thought.

"And Charlene is working on a hat. It will have to be cardboard, but with the gold braid.... Oh, and Shiz Ota says she can make drawstring pants out of sheets, and if you starch them enough, they'll look fine.... Ruth, you'll have uniforms," he said desperately. "You can go."

Ruth started to laugh, "Freddy, you're crazier than I am. You're even crazier than Mr. Mundorf. Let's see these things. Put one on." She pulled one out, too, and he helped her struggle into it, resting his hands on her shoulders for a minute, longing to button it down the front for her. Ruth's face colored under his gaze. She fumbled with her buttons.

Neither Ruth nor Freddy was actually a size "small." The tunics were dazzling white cotton with a high collar and buttons all the way down the right front panel. They buttoned them as best they could; then Freddy marched around the box playing an imaginary trombone and humming "Stars and Stripes Forever." Freddy knew an "allegro, con brio" when he saw one. Ruth fell in step behind him singing the flute descant. Mr. Mundorf closed the door to the auditorium quietly and went out the back way smiling, shaking his head.

"Ruth, they're throwing a fund raiser for the band January 28th."

"Who's they?" Ruth was breathless from the marching and from Freddy's hands on her shoulders.

"Oh, you know, Caroline and Janet and Josephine..., all those women with the soft smiles and the sharp teeth."

"Freddy Noble," Ruth said laughing, "that's catty."

"No, they're a great bunch. It's that they want me to ask you... to take you...."

Ruth felt as if she'd been sideswiped. She turned away to hide her face and began to struggle out of her pharmacist's tunic. "And you don't want to," she said, concentrating on her buttons.

"No," Freddy said miserably. "No, I was planning to ask you, but I don't like the idea of.... matchmaking and all....It puts us both in a ...."

And you have no intention of getting mixed up with me, Ruth thought. And your son hates me, Ruth thought. Well, I have news, Freddy Noble, Ruth said to herself, as she worked furiously on her buttons, I have enough children during the day. I don't need another dose at night. She folded her tunic carefully and put it back in the box. And just because you're the only man in town who can carry a tune, she said to herself, that doesn't give you any special privileges with me, Freddy Noble.

"I make it a rule to drive myself to these shindigs, Freddy," she said, trying to keep her voice level. "You know that, and so do they. Help me lug these things back to my office. They'll make great uniforms. Two Sloughs Elementary is indebted to you." If she sounded brusque, so be it.

She thanked him again at her office door, watched him searching awkwardly for something to say to her, but there was no need. There was no need at all. "I'll get in touch with Shiz Ota first thing tomorrow," she said. "We'll have to get going on these right away."

"Yeah, sure," said Freddy, and he turned and fled.

Ruth closed her office door and burst into tears.

Freddy spent the rest of the afternoon tidying up shelves in the pharmacy. The more disheveled his emotions got, the more meticulous his pharmacy became. Freddy always put his foot in it with Ruth. Whatever he started out to say always came out swallowed. He had trouble talking to women, come to that. He swept a shelf full of glass pill bottles into a box and began to rearrange them. He stopped with a pill bottle held in mid-air.

What had he said to his wife Molly six years ago? Why had she raced into the night, simply raced, as if she were escaping a cage, nothing but a thin cardigan on her, that thin green cardigan that looked so muddy and drenched later. They wanted him to take it, but he wouldn't. "No," he said, "nothing." Not even her wedding ring. And he could see they thought that he blamed her. But he knew whose fault it was; not hers. It was only that he didn't want them mangling those poor swollen fingers that weren't even hers anymore.

What had he said to drive Molly out into that night? Her fine, ferocious face, her frenzied eyes. She had snatched up her cardigan, torn open the door, left it swinging wide open, plunged out into the dark. "I have to get out of here," she'd said.

"Be careful, that's all," he'd begged her. He hadn't even tried to stop her. Her desperation had overwhelmed him. He hadn't said, "I love you." He hadn't said, "I can't live without you," although he had ached with fear to see her rush out like that, into the fog, furious and wild.

Where had she gone? To play bridge, she'd said, but Freddy never found out where. Then afterwards he didn't want to know. He rebuffed attempts to shed light on the accident. When he had started telephoning around midnight, nobody knew of any bridge game. Awakened out of sound sleep, the town's responses had been cruelly incredulous. Maybe if he had started calling earlier, if he had alerted the sheriff sooner, maybe someone would have spotted the skid marks.

By the next morning he knew something terrible had happened. But she was high strung. The tule fog got to everybody sooner or later. Maybe she'd run off. "Dear God," he prayed, "let her have run off." "With a man, even," he prayed. He held Lionel and prayed that Molly had driven off to San Francisco to have herself a time.

Freddy called her parents in San Francisco. The sheriff issued a missing persons report with a description of the car. Nothing turned up. If only they knew where she was headed. The men looked at Freddy as if he should have known, should have kept a tighter rein on her, as if she were some nervous filly. A week went by, and Freddy hardly knew whether it was day or night. The town was socked in. The fog never lifted. Lionel wandered around the house in his sleepers, his padded feet and his dragged blanket making a soft, sweeping sound. Lionel sat on the floor in corners and looked up at the legs of the strangers who trooped through the house. He crouched in corners in his dirty sleepers, sucking his blanket and his thumb.

Rumors began to circulate around town. Freddy watched them pickle the prim, pitying faces of the women who dropped off meat loafs and macaroni and cheese casseroles. None of the women knew for sure, but Molly was such a wild little mare, never really settled down in Two Sloughs, not really. The crop duster's name came up. Freddy hated those sympathetic, smug womanly faces most of all. Why did women turn on each other so softly? Why didn't they just gouge each other's eyes out, he wondered. He got so he wouldn't answer the door.

Nothing was ever said directly to Freddy. Even after Ben Heimann finally noticed the skid marks on the levee road above the Steamboat Slough Bridge. Even after they decided to drag the river. Even after they wouldn't let him come to see until after they'd cleaned her up some. But the car was still coated with mud and slime. Her hair was so full of mud and weeds it didn't even look red anymore. The fire in that flaming red hair had been doused. It was sodden, slimy. It felt like old weeds to his touch. How could the river dissolve so vivid a creature, so concentrate a woman? There was nothing in that bloated lump even to remember her by.

The sheriff told him she'd hit her head. Probably never felt a thing. But he would have said that. Freddy guessed it was his job to say things like that. A week in the river is a long time. Maybe nobody could have told for sure.

He hadn't even tried to stop her. He hadn't even yelled after her, "I love you."

Freddy looked at the pill bottle he held in his hand as if he'd never seen it before.

Ruth was ready for Charlene when she called. "What a great idea. A Tule Fog Party. Oh, no, thanks anyway, tell him not to bother. I always drive myself to parties in Two Sloughs."

"You know," said Charlene, "there's such a thing as being too independent."

"Independent?" Ruth thought as she hung up the telephone. Is that what it is when a guy won't touch you with a ten foot pole? Ruth mulled the word over: "Independent." Well, she thought, it beats "unattractive." It sure beats "old maid." What had her sister Jeanie called her? "Frigid?"

Charlene didn't tell Ruth what Old Man Bream had called her when Charlene went up to ask him for a donation to the Two Sloughs Band Uniform Fund.

"That man's really mean," Charlene told Larry.

"Now, I warned you," Larry said.

"I know. But why take out all his spite on the kids? He'd do anything to hurt Ruth."

"It doesn't help that Ruth's so feisty."

"What's she supposed to do? Take it on the chin?"

The river was still high. But Ruth couldn't see it for the fog. In fact she couldn't see the trees that lined the riverbanks or the edge of the pavement either. Ruth had never seen the fog this bad. She crept home after school in her car with the headlights on. In the middle of the day. The minute she left the school it vanished in the fog. The moment she passed a car on the road, it disappeared. She had the creepy feeling that the town was being erased behind her. As soon as the rain had let up, this clammy fog had blanketed the delta like some waterlogged shroud. It seeped under doorjambs, under overcoats, under your skin, chilling your bones. It muffled sound; it doused light. It blurred the difference between night and day. It was a terrible night to throw a party.

Ruth had bought a new dress for the Tule Fog Party, which made no sense, really. Her brown silk dress would have been fine, but Charlene talked her into it.

"It's too gray a month to wear brown. Let's find you a little color for a change," Charlene urged, and she'd talked Ruth into a burgundy red wool dress with a rhinestone button at the neck. She even made Ruth buy a new lipstick to match.

"It's only a P.T.A. meeting, more or less," complained Ruth.

"It's a party," said Charlene. "Lighten up."

Charlene had a good eye. Ruth didn't own a full length mirror, but the night of the party she stood on her bed in her stocking feet, viewing most of herself in the mirror over her dresser. She had to admit that Charlene had picked out a becoming dress. She twisted around so she could see the back. She didn't look quite so fat in this dress, and the color was flattering.

She got down off the bed. Her hair had frizzed up in the fog. It's only another P.T.A. meeting, more or less, she reassured herself. Then she fished around in her top bureau drawer for a pair of rhinestone earrings that had been her mother's. Was it too much glitter? She was being ridiculous. She slammed the bureau drawer, grabbed her coat, which was two inches too short, and stomped out the door to her car.

She was frightened even driving to the party. She had the uneasy feeling that the Tule Fog Party was somehow to blame for the weather. The party was held at Doc and Caroline Grahams' house in the center of Lambert Tract, the "white" section of town, which meant that only a few of the Chinese and Japanese parents would show up.

Caroline Graham met Ruth at the door and took her too-short coat, "Why, Ruth, you look lovely. Why, you look just like one of those shiny red Christmas balls. Come on in."

Ruth's knees buckled. Shiny red Christmas ball? Damn Charlene! Damn … but Doc appeared beside Caroline at that moment. Ruth straightened up (A shiny red Christmas ball!) and went into the living room with him. Freddy came up to her, "Hi, Ruth. You look great." Freddy blushed, embarrassed by his outburst.

"Yeah, if you like Christmas tree ornaments," Ruth snapped.

Oh, Lord. What had he done now? Why had he popped up with a crack like that. He'd meant it to be a compliment. He wasn't used to giving compliments. It was only that Ruth had looked pretty standing under the hall light, kind of shining. Freddy backed off as if Ruth had bitten him, his eyes filled with panic.

Charlene watched the exchange between Freddy and Ruth from the other end of the living room. She wandered over. "What did you say to Freddy?" Charlene asked. "He turned tail as if you'd taken a ruler to him."

"Oh, nothing," Ruth said. "Caroline says I look like a damned Christmas tree ball in this dress."

"She would. She doesn't like anybody stealing the spotlight from her. Vindictive little bitch. You look fabulous. Those earrings are perfect. I've got to get my cheese balls out of the oven."

Charlene's sassy assurances cheered her, but she still felt strangely rattled. She had to admit that Caroline Graham had gone to a lot of trouble for the party. She'd cleared out furniture to make room for everybody. She'd cut musical notes out of construction paper and taped them to the walls. She'd covered her table with a damask tablecloth and brought out her mother's solid silver punch bowl from Charleston, South Carolina. All of Lambert

Tract showed up, even on this rotten night. Ruth was touched by the town's support. She went to work trying to talk to parents, to come up with some positive little comment about the first grader whose only distinguishing achievement so far had been to wet his pants the first day of school.

Ping Lowe brought his pork rolls and his punch, but Ruth noticed that he didn't bring his wife. He left all the extra mixings for the punch under the table, and slipped out early. Shiz Ota and her husband came and Tosh and Fuji Nakamura, but they pleaded fear of driving in the fog. They didn't stay long.

Ruth caught Freddy looking at her a couple of times, but he dropped his gaze as soon as their eyes met. Maybe she had been a little snappish. He looked handsome tonight in a navy blazer, white shirt and striped silk tie. She started to approach him once, but he and Doc were in some serious discussion, so she didn't want to interrupt. Then she realized that most of the men had gravitated to the far end of the living room, where they leaned against the wall with their arms folded, or stood, legs slightly apart, heads down, as if they were literally kicking the conversation around with their feet. They reminded her of third graders lined up in the boys' bathroom.

The women clustered around the fireplace, keeping one eye on the men at the far end of the room and interrupting each other with tidbits of gossip. Ruth hesitated in the middle of the room. She didn't seem to belong in either group. She stuck out like a sore thumb, a bright red Christmas ornament, alone in the center of the room, next to the cheese balls.

Freddy's son Lionel was spending the night at Ricky Scoleri's house next door to the Grahams. Freddy had arranged it, thinking it would be safer to have him right next door, thinking maybe Ruth would let him drive her home because of the fog. Maybe they could stop at Joe's Bar for a night cap even. He hadn't really thought it out, but Ricky Scoleri's mother said that would be fine, the boys could sleep in Hopalong Cassidy sleeping bags in the living room and she'd make them French toast for breakfast.

Lionel and Ricky showed up at the Graham's kitchen door part way through the party, which made the Graham girls mad. The boys sneaked in, looked over the buffet table and the punch bowl. But it was getting crowded. Even Ruth didn't notice them. When they crawled under the buffet table, where Ping had stored all the extra punch ingredients, the Graham girls threatened to tell their mother. While the girls ran off to find her, Lionel crawled out, glanced wickedly around, poured a whole bottle of rum into the punch and scooted out the back door.

Caroline Graham loved a good party. She told the girls to offer the boys a coke and a meatball. But they had to stay in the kitchen, she said, and so did the girls. Caroline looked around for the boys, couldn't see them, ladled another glass of punch for Freddy Noble, then one for herself and forgot all about them.

The room became so crowded that it was hard to move around. Ruth was too short to see Freddy at all. She was pinned next to the fireplace learning about the mysterious flooding in the Martin's basement. Suddenly she heard his voice. He was singing. Freddy was singing. Two-part harmony, "Side by Side." With whom? Ruth subtly craned her neck, but the singers were hidden in the crush. The room had become stifling hot.

"I've got to get some fresh air," Ruth pleaded finally. "This dress is too hot."

"It's a gorgeous dress," Janet Martin said. "Where did you find it?"

Ruth wormed her way through the crowd, chatting politely as she went, then moving on, pleading thirst. The duet grew louder. Stephen Foster songs. Freddy's accompanying soprano was singing sharp. It must be Caroline Graham.

Doc Graham stopped her, asked about her Christmas. He seemed oblivious to the fact that his wife Caroline was singing sharp. Ruth told Doc about her new kitten. "What do you know about spaying cats?" she asked.

"Not enough," Doc said. "I tried to spay Jenny's cat and killed it. It was probably the low point in my medical career. She still hasn't forgiven me."

Ruth laughed in spite of herself. He looked so chagrined.

"The operation was a success, but I messed up on the anesthetic. Overestimated. My hot shot gynecologist friend from San Francisco assisted. John Boynton. He was up here duck hunting one Sunday. It was awful," he moaned. "There we were by ourselves in the office, probably twenty years of medical training between us, trying to resuscitate a damn cat. We tried everything -- electric shock, open heart massage.... Take your cat up to Sacramento to a vet. That's my advice."

All the time Ruth could hear Freddy singing, could hear the giggling accompaniment of a squeaky soprano beside him.

Charlene came up with a cup of punch for Doc. "Caroline's into two-part harmony tonight," she said and laughed. She held the cup up to him. Doc sighed. As he took the cup from Charlene, Charlene gently stroked the side of his hand, looked into his eyes. "You O.K.?" she asked softly.

Suddenly Ruth didn't want to be there, standing between Charlene and Doc while nobody said anything. It seemed too crowded all of a sudden, too loud. Ruth backed away muttering something about getting some punch herself, but Charlene and Doc didn't even hear her.

Freddy's voice soared over the crowd, "Ooooklahoma..." She needed to find him, to regain her balance somehow. She elbowed her way through the press of parents, headed for the sound of his voice. She found him at the punch bowl. With Caroline Graham all over him. All that singing had made them thirsty apparently. Caroline curled her arm around Freddy's shoulder while Freddy attempted to fill their cups. She wasn't helping. Freddy was spilling quite a lot. That southern charm of Caroline's was oozing out all over the place. Not that Ruth cared. She took a deep breath and approached the punch bowl.

"Ruth," Freddy said. His face lit up, "I was looking for you. Your party's drawn quite a crowd."

This is <u>maaah</u> party, Honey," interrupted Caroline, her southern accent thickening, "and this is <u>maaah</u> man. Go find yo'self anuthu man." And she put her arms around Freddy's neck and kissed him hard on the mouth, causing him to stagger backwards. Freddy Noble was drunk as a skunk!

Ruth looked on in horror while Caroline unsteadily guided Freddy into a chair beside the punch bowl, then sat on his lap, draping herself around him, offering him sips of punch from her cup, kissing him, crooning to him about what a wonderful "singah" he was. Freddy kept looking at Ruth with a glassy expression on his face and singing. All the songs from "Oklahoma." Even in his drunken condition, he sang on key, but he made a hash of the lyrics. When he got to "People will say we're in love," his tongue disintegrated. Ruth couldn't stand it any more.

She turned away to find Charlene's husband Larry standing right behind her, with his arms crossed, surveying the scene. Doc was still off in the corner with Charlene, their heads bowed, nearly touching, deep in conversation. Larry studied Doc and his wife, then turned and watched Freddy and Caroline for a minute or two. Finally Larry filled a glass from the punch bowl and sniffed it. Then he tasted it. "Whew," he said. "Dynamite." He picked up the punch bowl and disappeared into the kitchen with it, to the dismay of Caroline and Freddy, who were guzzling their punch happily.

"Sorry about that, Ruth," Larry said when he came back out of the kitchen. "Somebody spiked the punch."

"It's not <u>my</u> problem," said Ruth, a shade too vehemently. "Who did it?"

"The girls say it must have been Lionel. There's a quart of 151 proof rum in the kitchen wastebasket."

"Whew!"

"It could have happened to anybody, Ruth."

"But it didn't," said Ruth acidly.

"Right," agreed Larry disgustedly. "I'm getting Charlene the hell out of here. We're going home," said Larry.

Ruth looked at Larry, shocked by the fury in his voice, confused by the exchange she'd witnessed between Doc and Charlene. She felt guilty without knowing why, hurt for no real reason. She felt left over, like a round red Christmas ball too long after Christmas.

She watched Larry stride over to Doc and Charlene, shove Doc back a step, put his arm around Charlene's shoulder, and, speaking under his breath, guide her toward the front door. The party melted back out of Larry's way. Janet Martin started to say, "Leaving so soon?" But the words died on her lips when she saw the expression on Larry's face.

The heavy silence that followed Charlene and Larry's departure was interrupted by a loud thump. Freddy Noble had keeled over sideways out of his chair, dumping Caroline from his lap onto the floor. Caroline shrieked and came up onto her hands and knees with a bloody nose that soaked the front of her pale peach charmeuse. Freddy was out like a light. It took three men to get him up. As they neared the front door carrying Freddy, Dan Martin looked out from under Freddy's right shoulder and said, "Shut up, Janet." After this second departure there was no use pretending. The gaiety had fizzled out of the party. The rest of the town tried to carry on as if nothing had happened, but they gave it up. One by one, they pleaded thick fog, said goodnight, shoved some bills into the coffee can by the door and vanished into the gloom.

Ruth offered to help Doc clean up (Caroline had disappeared,) but she couldn't look him in the eye. He said, no, thanks, they'd leave it 'til tomorrow. She retrieved her too-short coat and left him slumped wearily in a chair by the fire, nursing a glass of brandy. She wasn't sure he'd even noticed her leave.

She drove home slowly, afraid she'd miss her road in the fog, feeling off kilter, as if she were losing her bearings, feeling miserable. She couldn't say why, really. Freddy Noble was a fool, probably a lonesome fool. Caroline Graham was a problem, possibly a lonesome problem. God only knew what was wrong with Doc. It had nothing to do with Ruth. So why was she sitting in bed, wrapped up in one of her mother's Afghans as if she were coming down with something, holding Clarinet and feeling sorry for herself? "This tule fog gets to you after a while," she said to the kitten. "I should go away for Lincoln's Birthday."

Charlene dropped by the next morning with a warm loaf of cracked wheat bread. "I know how you feel," she said.

"I feel fine," said Ruth. I didn't drink any punch."

"Freddy made an ass of himself."

"I don't care a damn what Freddy Noble does. Why does everybody think I care? I feel sorry for Doc, is all."

"Don't feel sorry for Doc. He gets plenty of commiseration on the side."

"Charlene, that's a mean, ugly rumor to start. That's not like you."

"It's not a rumor because I'm the one he's fooling around with. It's not a rumor because I don't expect it to go any further. It is mean because I'm feeling mean. And sorry for myself. It's this damn fog."

"What! How did you...?" Ruth felt as if the whole town was sinking into the mud, as if the floor beneath her feet was turning soggy.

"Oh, I don't know. I guess it was partly this cancer thing. And spending a lot of time at the office. And Doc being sympathetic. Larry won't talk about it. The cancer, I mean. He hates the whole subject. And me seeing my life go by, not wanting to die, wondering what else is there? I don't know. It was dumb. Doc told me flat out that he would never leave Caroline. And God, Larry's been my best friend since high school, except for Mavis. I don't think I even like Doc. He thinks too much. He never loses himself. Larry's just a slob, but he's a warm, friendly slob, you know? No, maybe you don't know. Find a warm one, Ruth, one with a sense of humor. That's my advice."

"Why would I even want one. They're all a bunch of jerks.So is it over?" Ruth asked.

"Yeah, I guess that's why I'm here. I guess I knew if I said it out loud, it would sound so stupid and sordid.... I knew I could trust you to ....Sorry to throw it at you when you're feeling down in the dumps already."

"Charlene, I'm not down in the dumps. There's nothing going on between Freddy and me."

"Well, there should be," said Charlene.

"Well, there isn't," said Ruth testily.

"Well, with the whole town ganging up on you, it's no wonder."

Ruth sat at her kitchen table and watched Charlene disappear into the fog. It seemed to her that the tule fog had dissolved the town some way, turned it to soup. Clarinet was yowling at the kitchen door. Ruth opened the door to let her in and found her standing proudly over a dead mouse, her first catch. "Oh, yuck, Clarinet, what a disgusting habit. What is this anyway, the Year of the Rat?"

"So who hasn't gotten drunk and danced on a table once in his life?" Caroline Graham asked when she telephoned later that morning to tell Ruth how much money they had made on the party.

"What do I care where he dances?" said Ruth. "The numbskull."

"I got a little carried away myself," said Caroline.

"You were sandbagged, Caroline, by that nasty kid of his."

"Oh, Ruth, it wasn't only that. Things have been rocky with Doc and me lately. I guess you'd gathered that."

Ruth had the panicky feeling that Caroline thought she knew something, "Doc's a good guy, Caroline."

"That's what everybody says" said Caroline exasperated, "the whole blasted town. He's a damned God around here. For him Two Sloughs is a little heaven. Not for me. I just try to remind him every once in a while that he's human. That's all." Her voice broke. "So am I."

"Men," muttered Ruth sympathetically.

"Not only men, Ruth. Nobody's perfect. In fact, being perfect could get pretty lonesome."

Who's she talking about, thought Ruth after she hung up the phone.

Jimmy and Sally Martin couldn't figure out their parents at breakfast the morning after the Tule Fog Party. They were real grumpy. They were having an argument, but they didn't want Jimmy and Sally to know what it was about, so they talked in parents' code:

"She always was trouble," Janet huffed as she buttered the toast.

"He got pie-eyed!" Dan retorted.

"Why Doc didn't...."

"He was busy himself over in that...."

"You should talk! You...." Janet looked around the kitchen and stopped mid-sentence, turned her back on her husband, "You do the toast."

Jimmy and Sally gave each other the "mean shark" look that meant, "Lie low. Keep your mouth shut."It all seemed to have something to do with the Tule Fog Party.

After breakfast, Sally said, "Ride over to Lionel's and find out what happened."

But Freddy met Jimmy at the door. His face was grim. "Lionel is grounded. He can't play."

"O.K.," said Jimmy, "Tell him to come over when he's out."

"He's not going to be out. Ever again," said Freddy, and he slammed the door.

"Hoooo, man," Jimmy whistled through his teeth as he rode home. What did he do? Burn down a house? Jimmy had seen his own parents mad. They got over it. And usually one of them was less mad at him than the other one, so he had this kind of grouchy ally. But Lionel had only one parent, Freddy, and Jimmy had never seen Freddy this mad before.

February

Ruth didn't want to go to Ike's. It had nothing to do with Freddy Noble. She just didn't feel like making small talk. She was too busy. But her worst fears about Mr. Mundorf's sailing ship were coming true. It was magnificent. It cut through the white and turquoise blue cardboard waves, right across the middle of the stage, paper flags flying, paper mache figurehead gleaming. It was a beautiful bark. But it wasn't safe. Carl Mundorf was a heck of an artist, but he wasn't much of a naval architect. The deck, upon which the entire fourth grade was supposed to stand, lurched dangerously. The bamboo masts wobbled. The yards of main sail and mizzen sail and jib that Mr. Mundorf had cajoled from the mothers of Two Sloughs (there couldn't be a sheet left in town, by Ruth's estimate) kept coming down and enveloping the chorus. Ruth needed help, and she knew it.

"Come in out of the cold, Ruth. Surprised you could find the door." Sausage sizzled behind Ike on the griddle. His bald head was rosy from the heat of the stove. Ike had a genius for making you feel comfortable.

She smiled at him, took the mug of coffee he offered her. "Wasn't easy," she said. "It's thicker this morning than yesterday."

"It's supposed to start raining again. That should break it up some."

"Let's hope so." Her gaze strayed down the counter.

"I hear the band is sounding great," Freddy said from the other end of the counter.

Ruth hadn't seen Freddy since the Tule Fog party. She had stayed away from the pharmacy. She kept her voice absolutely even, "Except for those darned clarinets. Lionel's coming along on that trombone, though." A note of surprise crept into her voice.

Dan Martin laughed. "He should be. All that practice he's getting."

"Practice?" Ruth was genuinely stumped.

"That's what I heard," Dan said chuckling. "Poor kid."

"Less than he deserves, the little rat," said Harvey Lemmon, laughing.

Mystified, Ruth looked down the counter at Freddy. Freddy scowled, studied his coffee cup. Ruth looked at Dan.

"He had it coming," Dan said. "It was Lionel spiked the punch at the party. 151 proof rum. Damn near brought the town down around him."

"So what happened?" she asked

The men stared at her in silent, open-mouthed amazement.

"I mean to Lionel?" she added hastily.

"He's grounded," Freddy said gruffly. "He's too old for that stuff. He could have hurt somebody."

"You haven't been into the pharmacy, I guess. Lionel's in the back from 3:00 until 5:00 every day practicing trombone."

"Business tapered off some in the afternoon, Freddy?" asked Ben Heimann, laughing.

"Don't care if it has," Freddy said tersely.

Ruth could see that Freddy was angry. The men had seen it, too, thought maybe they'd gone too far.

"O.K., Ben, Harvey," said Ike, "fried egg sandwiches with bacon. This here's the runny yolk, that one's the hard yolk. Who has which?"

"Runny, that's me," said Harvey.

"How's the Music Festival coming, Ruth?" Ben asked, grateful to have been let off the hook with Freddy.

"Fine," Ruth said. "The kids are working hard." She took another sip of coffee. "We've got a little trouble with the sets," she said, trying to sound casual about it. "Mr. Mundorf isn't too strong on the structural side."

Louie chuckled, "I'll never forget that windmill if I live to be a hundred."

The men laughed. "We had half the fathers on stage before that was over, holding the damn thing up," Dan said. "Nobody should let Carl Mundorf near a refrigerator carton, much less three of them, one on top of the other."

"What have we got this time," Ben asked, "the Eiffel Tower? The Golden Gate Bridge?"

Ruth was thrown by Freddy's brusqueness with the men. Why was Freddy so testy? Why had he come down so hard on Lionel? Was he mad at her too? She found herself staring down to the far end of the counter at the top of Freddy's head. He was real intent on the handle of his coffee cup. Then she noticed to her chagrin that all the heads lined up along the counter between Freddy and herself were turned toward her. The men were all looking at her expectantly. Obviously somebody had asked her a question. They were waiting for an answer.

"What do you need, Ruth?" Dan prompted gently.

"Well, I'm not sure," said Ruth, flustered. It wasn't her fault Freddy'd made a fool of himself at the party. "You see, it's a boat, a ship actually, a three masted, square-rigged man of war," she said miserably, "and it's wobbly as all heck."

"This sounds like a job for Clarence Henderson," Ben said. "He's got extension ladders. I'll give him a call. After school O.K.? You free, Dan?"

"Sure," Dan said.

"I knew it involved sheets," Harvey complained. "It's gettin' hard to go to bed around our house."

"And there's damned little else to do around here this time of year," said Joe Scoleri. "Beggin' your pardon, Ruth."

Ruth could feel the men squirm at this remark. They thought it was too off-color for mixed company. It was time for her to go. She waited a moment or two so that she wouldn't appear to have taken offense. She would have almost welcomed an occasional dirty joke. Sometimes she felt like the Vestal Virgin of Two Sloughs, protected, isolated. If these guys knew what their kids piped up with in the second grade.... She probably knew more about the love lives of Two Sloughs than anybody besides Doc.

"Clarinet caught her first mouse, Louie. Thanks."

"Good. Good. Bad year for mice. Rats, too," said Louie.

You can say that again, thought Ruth. She finished her coffee and rose, "Thanks, Ike." She turned to the row of men, "I'll see you after school then. Thanks." Every head turned toward her a quarter turn except Freddy's.

She sat in her car with the motor running and the heater on. So Freddy had finally let Lionel have it. Well, she'd been telling him to do it for years. Why had this incident triggered such strong punishment? Had he always been attracted to Caroline Graham? Had he scared himself? Did he think he had offended Doc? Or Ruth? It was none of her affair. It wasn't like Freddy to be so surly.

She'd best drive off, she thought, or somebody would come out of Ike's to ask if she had car trouble. She turned her headlights on and headed back to school in the fog. She had been more upset by Freddy's behavior at the party than she wanted to admit. She told herself that she disliked drunkenness. But the image that stuck in her mind was of Freddy kissing Caroline passionately on the lips as she sat in his lap.

Out of the corner of his eye Ike watched Ruth walk out to her car, saw her shoulders slump a little, saw her face turn away as if she'd been slapped. Over the years Ike had become a kind of an expert on the way people walked in and out of his place. Nearly every problem in Two Sloughs had come up for discussion at Ike's. But because the town was small and his customers were mostly men, the talk was all banked shots, aimed obliquely. Ike depended a lot on the hunch of the shoulders, the weight of the walk, the cast of the eyes to tell him the rest of the story. He didn't like what he saw. Freddy had been downright cold toward Ruth, and Ruth had felt it. Ike was no matchmaker. He knew better. But this was a bad sign. He put up an order of sausage and scrambled, filled coffee cups. When he got to Freddy's cup at the far end of the counter, he said quietly, "Sounds like Lionel might have some talent in the music department."

"I don't know. He hates it," Freddy mumbled.

"They all do," Ike said. "But if he's good at it, it could be the making of him."

"Naw, he and Ruth don't get along," Fred said.

"Ruth's fair, Fred. She gives everybody a chance." Ike had wandered off up the counter filling cups, stacking plates, before Freddy could reply. Ike would have to talk this over with Emma.

Ike's wife Emma was wheelchair bound. She got polio when she was eighteen, the most beautiful girl on the river, then and now, Ike thought. Big black eyes, long lashes. Ike's was only open for breakfast and lunch. By the time Ike got home at 3:00, Emma had herself up, bathed and dressed, and she'd done most of the housework. That girl was a wonder. Ike and Ben Heimann had rigged up a series of pulleys and bars all over the house. They had widened the doors, knocked out a wall or two. It astounded Ike what she came up with. She'd learned to work the vacuum from her chair. She'd fashioned a hook for the upper shelves and a duster on a long pole. Her smile just about lit up the house. Ike could hardly wait to come home to it. He filled her in on the day and the gossip, the goings on about town. He retold all the funny stories, imitating perfectly the men who sat at his counter until Emma could see the whole scene as if she had been perched up on the hat rack. The men of Two Sloughs would have been amazed to see this stolid figure, dancing around his living room, grabbing hold of a standing lamp to use as a prop, pulling a hat down over his face, acting out their foibles and follies for his wife. He even told her the least raunchy of the dirty jokes. She laughed until tears came to her eyes.

Ike would discuss this Fred situation with Emma when he got home. The man had gotten drunk and made a pass at Caroline Graham, apparently. But Caroline Graham was a prick teaser from way back. Emma had spotted it right off. Caroline wanted more than Two Sloughs had to offer. Emma had seen that brooding, unsatisfied look in Doc's eyes, too. Freddy was going to have to forget about the whole incident. Doc and Caroline were surely anxious to forget about it. The town didn't want to dwell on it. Well, they did, but it was the kind of subject that could remain publicly closed but much discussed in double beds around town after the children were asleep.

The thing was, Freddy was hurting Ruth. Ike and Emma felt protective of Ruth. Maybe because they didn't have children of their own. Maybe because Ruth had always come instinctively to Ike's for help. Ike and Emma would have to discuss it tonight.

Ruth pulled up in front of Two Sloughs Elementary and sat for a moment before she shut off the motor. Even though the whole Caroline Graham incident had upset her in confusing ways, it had never occurred to her until this morning that she might have lost Freddy's friendship over it. It wasn't a big romantic thing, but she would miss the music and the... well, fellowship. She thought of the afternoon they had sat on counter stools singing songs from "Oklahoma." The tunes rattled around in her head. "There's a bright golden haze on the meadow."   She thought of him lugging all those silly pharmacists' tunics down the hall. She felt bereft. It didn't seem fair.

She listened more carefully during band practice that day. By damn, Lionel was playing well. He had a good sense of rhythm, and his tone was getting much better.

"Lionel," she said after practice, "I'd like you to take a stab at that 'Semper Fidelis' solo Tommy Randolph is working on. I'm not sure you can do it, but it's supposed to be a duet. I'll transpose a copy of the music for you."

Lionel gave her a lidded, resentful look. Ruth had the creepy feeling that Lionel considered her responsible for his penance. What was it about that family? Why did they insist on blaming Ruth for all their problems? She had better find out what happened to those pharmacists' tunics, by the way. They were still signed up for the State Band Competition, and she was banking on dressing the band in the tunics for the Two Sloughs Music Festival, as well. A bunch of midget pharmacists playing "The Stars and Stripes Forever." She sighed. They'd look clean, anyway.

"How are we coming along with Lionel Noble?" With an unerring sense of timing Ursula Brown, the District child psychologist was on the telephone following up on their September discussion.

"Better, better," lied Ruth. "He seems to be taking to the trombone. I think I may be getting through to him."

"And his father?" Ursula asked smoothly.

"His father's finally coming down on him harder, too."

"I mean, how are you and the father communicating?"

"It hasn't been necessary," Ruth said stiffly.

"It would seem advisable to keep a pretty steady line of communication open between you and the father..." Ursula paused, "for the boy's sake."

"Yes, well, that's not in the cards right now, Ursula. The father's not speaking to me."

"Oh?"

"He seems to blame me for his getting drunk and making an ass of himself."

"Tell me about it."

"That whole family seems to blame me for their problems. Both of them, I mean. Look, Ursula, I've got a sinking ship on my hands. Could I call you back on this? Maybe after the Music Festival. I'll come up for dinner."

Ben and Dan Martin and Clarence Henderson arrived at 3:10, and by 4:30 they had thrown enough two by fours into Mr. Mundorf's sailing ship to hold up the fourth grade. They had tied the masts to the ceiling of the auditorium with about sixty yards of baling wire.

"The rafters will have to give before those masts come down," Ben promised. "I hope you didn't want to move that boat none."

Ruth gulped. She had been planning to push it forward on the stage, but she kept her mouth shut. The fourth graders would just have to sing out, that's all. She thanked the men and drove over to Shiz Ota's house in Japan Town to see how the uniform business was progressing.

In Shiz's small, tidy living room four women sat on dinette set chairs, sewing gold buttons on the tunics and chattering in Japanese. The bitter, grassy smell of green tea lingered in the room. A small altar was crowded with figurines and vases. Buddhist family altars in Two Sloughs had a familiar, cluttered domesticity to them -- a newspaper clipping, incense sticks, a trucker's cap, a ripe tangerine on a lacquer tray.

A single shelf held Shiz's ningyo, her doll. Shiz was a doll maker, an ancient Japanese art. Ruth examined the doll. The doll's costume was exquisite, her obi lovingly folded, her wig perfectly combed. Shiz had only sons, a blessing in a Japanese household. Ruth suspected this ningyo was her longed-for daughter.

Shiz fussed over Ruth, bringing a chair from the kitchen, pouring her tea. "You must see a uniform that is finished," Shiz said, and brought out of the bedroom a dazzling white tunic with two rows of brass buttons down the front, heavy gold braid on the collar and cuffs, and gold and blue epaulets on the shoulders.

Ruth couldn't believe her eyes. "How in the world...?" she began....

Shiz and the other ladies laughed. "You must have scared that Mr. Yee real good," Mrs. Matsubara said. "He brought us yards and yards of gold braid. Won't take money. He say Harold in band."

"I didn't scare Mr. Yee. He plays the saxophone. So does Harold. But...." Ruth sputtered.

"They made so much money on the Tule Fog Party they had plenty of money for buttons," Shiz said. "We changed all the buttons. Then we sewed a second row down the front. Double breasted. See?"

"Some tunics still too big," Mrs. Matsubara said. "Some of those fourth graders too small. But not bad for home made, huh?"

"You mean you've fitted them all?"

"Oh, yeah. They got names in them. See?"

Ruth collapsed in her chair. "I can't believe you did this. They're beautiful. No other band in the state will have uniforms as elegant as these. How long have you been working on these?"

"Oh, it wasn't so bad," said Shiz. "A lot of women in this town sew."

"I tell you, that Ike's wife, that Emma, she real good sewer," Mrs. Matsubara said. "Doc's wife, too."

"Caroline has been here?"

"Every afternoon," Shiz said. "You know, I like her. She's not the snob I thought she was. She brings the cookies. Here, have one. They're good."

"Has Freddy Noble seen these?" Ruth asked with her mouth full.

"No," Shiz said.

"Could I borrow one, to show him? I'll bring it right back."

Shiz walked out with Ruth to her car.

"Shiz, how can I ever thank you?"

"Miss Hardy, our boys will go to university. I know it. That is my husband's dream. Because of you they will go. Every button, I say, 'Thank you, Miss Hardy.'"

"They're good boys, Shiz, smart, hard working. They'll get into the university all by themselves."

"No," Shiz said, "you start them on the right path. That is the most important thing. I wish... I wish my daughter could be here, too."

"I didn't know you ever had a daughter."

"In the camp. Hospital was no good. The doctor collapsed, passed out cold. Not his fault. He'd been on his feet forty-eight hours straight. The nurses did what they could. But when she finally came, she was so pale, so still...." Shiz turned away.

"Oh, Shiz..." Ruth touched her arm.

Shiz grasped Ruth's hand. Tears caught in the corners of her eyes. "I wish for you someday a daughter. It is the greatest gift, a daughter." Shiz squeezed her hand and went back in the house.

A daughter. Ruth sat staring at the drab house. A daughter. Ruth had been too knee-deep in children to think about having a daughter of her own. A daughter.

In fact, she'd always felt apologetic for not having been a son. But Shiz Ota meant what she said. "It is the greatest gift." A daughter. Had her mother felt that bond? Ruth remembered a morning at her mother's bedside shortly before her mother died. Her mother had been drifting in and out of consciousness. Ruth had been reading the paper when she felt her mother looking at her.

"Hi. You feeling any better?"

Her mother stared at her, appeared not to have heard her. Her mother's face had dried and flaked and fallen away until there was nothing left except her eyes.

"You'll be everything I ever wanted to be. I was always too scared to grab it. I blamed your father, but I was just too scared to grab it. Thank God, Ruthie."

Ruth sat in her car remembering her mother's ravaged, tender face. "I wish for you someday a daughter," Shiz had said. Ruth had never looked at it quite that way. Was that what made her mother push and bully her girls so badly? "Someday a daughter." Would she ever have a daughter of her own?

It was nearly closing time at the Two Sloughs Pharmacy. Josephine Lemmon had already left for the day, and Freddy was about to lock up. Ruth heard petulant trombone music coming from the back room.

"Freddy, have you got a minute? I wanted to show you something." She was breathless with excitement.

"Sure, Ruth. Anything wrong?"

"No. You mean with Lionel? No. Did he tell you I gave him a solo part? Sousa. It's a duet, actually, with Tommy Randolph."

"He said you didn't think he could do it." Freddy stayed back of the counter.

"That was only to trick him into trying." She couldn't stand it any longer. She brought out the uniform she had hidden behind her back and held it up, "Look."

Freddy stared at the uniform, thunderstruck, as if he couldn't believe this could be one of the pharmacist tunics he had bought for Ruth. He came out from behind the counter, examined it, caressed the fabric, his fingers close to Ruth's as they held the uniform together. "Incredible," he said at last. "Incredible," he said, laughing. "Shiz Ota did this?"

"She and a couple of dozen other women. They're nearly finished." Ruth clutched the uniform to her breast, bowed her head, admiring it. "Thank you, Freddy," she murmured.

Freddy covered Ruth's hand with his own. Ruth felt her breast beneath the uniform rise to the pressure of Freddy's hand. Freddy felt it, too. He brushed his hand across her collarbone and rested it lightly on her shoulder. The trombone playing stopped in the back room. The store went quiet.

"Ruth, I wondered if...."

A door creaked open.

"Can I stop now? It's five." Lionel trudged into the room, dragging his trombone, looked up, saw Ruth and froze.

Freddy dropped his hand from Ruth's shoulder, blushed beet red.

Lionel stood stock-still staring at the two adults.

Ruth pulled the uniform up to her chin and looked helplessly at Freddy. Freddy's eyes seemed locked on her face. A radiator pipe clanked.

"Yes," Freddy finally broke the silence. "Yes," he said hoarsely, without looking at Lionel, "Go pack up your instrument. And check the back door for me, will you?"

Lionel disappeared.

"Ruth," he said in a low voice, flustered, blushing. He couldn't seem to go on.

"I wanted you to see one, Freddy. You were right. We <u>could</u> do it. If we just tried. Shiz says the hats are sensational, too. Charlene really went to town apparently -- feathers, gold braid. She's real artistic, you know." Ruth was blathering, but she couldn't seem to stop herself. "She got Tommy Randolph's mother gluing gold sequins. Tommy's mom enlisted some of the girls from Mr. Yee's. Don't ask me how. Professional connections, maybe. I guess they had glue and sequins from one end of Charlene's kitchen to the other,"

Freddy laughed nervously, "That explains it," he said. "Larry says he's afraid to eat breakfast at home anymore. Afraid of what he'll find in his oatmeal."

"Sequins and feathers," said Ruth, "It seems they made so much money on that Tule Fog Party...." Oh, Lord, she wished she hadn't brought that up. The laughter vanished from Freddy's face.

"Yeah, well...." He lowered his head and slipped behind the counter again, started straightening the receipt books.

"Fred," Ruth reached out and touched his arm. "That could have happened to anybody."

"Yeah," He turned away, "But it didn't."

Ruth went home and built a fire with the pear wood prunings that Angelo Giannini always left on her back porch, cut to length. She felt cold and tired and discouraged. She wanted somebody else to build the fire for a change, to light it, to crumple up another piece of newspaper when it faltered, to bring her a drink by the fire, to ask about her day.

The minute she sat down in her big chair by the fire Clarinet sprang into Ruth's lap and pushed her head under Ruth's hand to be scratched. Ruth was envious. What she wanted was a lap to crawl into, "You're a sybarite, you know that?" Ruth scratched the top of Clarinet's head, behind her ears, "So Clarinet, what do you know about men?" She asked, gazing at the sputtering fire. "Here we've got Doc, who's the most decent guy in the world, cheating on his wife. We've got Freddy, who's the sweetest guy ever born, turned sullen and sulky. Arm's length. I'd say he's keeping me at arm's length." She stroked the cat, who purred and rolled over onto her side, "What do you make of it all, fat cat? You're the rat expert."

Finally, the fire blazed. It could use another log now, but Ruth sat staring into the flames. Men -- Doc, Freddy.... She could have added Edmund's name to her list, but she had never talked to anyone except Charlene about Edmund. And she'd glossed over the story to Charlene -- summer romance. She'd left out the hurt. They had met in Salzburg that storybook summer, ten years ago now, that summer between the wars. She was barely twenty-two. Two American music students on an exchange program. The music seduced them first. Edmund was a pianist. Ruth had come to sing. And music surrounded them: in the streets, in the churches, in the beer halls, in the mountains most of all. Children tending goats on the hillsides sang thin, wavering tunes about mountain brooks, silly hiking songs, songs that trailed off into rounds, tinkled with laughter. They laughed at the Nazi youth groups, called them "the operetta chorus," glossed over the post war poverty. (They were poor, too.) The Austrian countryside seemed untouched. They bicycled together through Alpen valleys filled with buttercups, took refuge in hay barns during summer showers, nicknamed each other Heidi and Peter. They felt enchanted.

Ruth and Edmund hoarded their meager allowances and bought standing room tickets to every concert. They dined afterward on a single piece of chocolate and whipped cream *kuchen* cut carefully in half. Edmund said she looked like an Austrian *mädchen*. He insisted she wear her dirndl, which revealed the shadow of her round breasts above the low cut white eyelet blouse. He wove buttercup wreaths for her hair. She felt plump and pretty and in love. Edmund was the star pupil in the summer program. It was he who was chosen to play at the end of the term concert. His bony fingers were long and ivory. When they explored her breasts, her hips, played between her legs, sounds came up from deep inside her that had nothing to do with any chromatic scale.

Then summer ended, that last summer before the war, and Edmund said goodbye. "There's no point in writing," he said. "We both have too many plans. Let's cut it off the way Goethe would have: short and sorrowful."

"Can't we even try?" she'd asked.

But Edmund was gifted and ambitious. He had his eye on Julliard. He took her to the train, gave her a bouquet of white and yellow field flowers, kissed her, followed along the platform waving goodbye. Then he turned and walked away. He never looked back. Not once. He meant it.

Ruth had written. She couldn't help it. For a few weeks she was afraid she might be pregnant. She didn't have his exact address, only the town on Long Island. She never received a reply. Even now, ten years later, she scanned the list of soloists coming to San Francisco every season, half-expecting to see Edmund's name. He wouldn't even try. He hadn't looked back. He had refused even to try. She couldn't get over that.

That compartmentalized love was still a mystery to Ruth. Edmund had loved her, she was sure. But he had been willing to turn away from her for the sake of his career. He would have said he saw the situation clearly. His career came first. She would have said that he suffered from tunnel vision, myopia, that he would suffer great unhappiness from looking at the world this way, that he would end up lonely and perhaps bitter.

Did all men look at the world through such a narrow focus? Did they have no "cat's whiskers," as her mother used to call them, no peripheral vision, no eyes in the back of their heads? Did they all barge straight ahead through life missing the peripheral dreams, the scattered hopes, the spilt affections?

Clarinet stretched contentedly in Ruth's lap, digging her claws into Ruth's thigh. "Ow," said Ruth. "Stop that." She stroked the kitten. "Your rats are less complicated, fat cat. They can't carry a tune."

A car pulled up in front, and Caroline Graham got out. Ruth hadn't been avoiding Caroline, exactly. She simply hadn't had any occasion to speak to her since the morning after the Tule Fog Party, and she really didn't feel like speaking to her now. She sighed, flipped Clarinet off her lap and tossed another log on the fire. On the other hand, Caroline had been sewing like a fiend on the band uniforms. Maybe it was just to impress Freddy, but the results were astounding.

"Caroline," Ruth said guiltily, opening the kitchen door. "I should have called you. Come in by the fire. I had no idea how much time you'd put in on the band uniforms."

"Shiz said you'd been by. Think of it as penance, Ruth." Caroline offered Ruth a red tin, "I brought you some cookies as a peace offering. I made an awful fool of myself at that party."

"Caroline, there's nothing between Freddy and me. Why..."

"I know. And it's partly my fault. And," she said gently, "you wish there were something between you."

Caroline had caught Ruth at a weak moment. The softness of Caroline's voice, the plainness of her apology crumpled Ruth. She sank into her chair, picked up Clarinet and hugged her, "I don't know, Caroline. Honestly, I don't know what I wish."

Caroline sat on the arm of her chair, "Don't let him get away, Ruth. Just because he made a mistake."

"He won't let me get within arm's reach of him."

"No." Caroline put a hand on her shoulder, patted her back the way her mother used to when she was unhappy. "And you're hurt. I nearly lost Doc because I was so hurt. And lonely and isolated. Being the doctor's wife in a town like this is like being the preacher's wife. Nobody talks to you. They're suspicious of what you know already. Because Doc knows them inside out, they suspect I do too. They sure aren't going to tell me any more."

"Doc loves you, Caroline."

"I know. I love him, too. He screwed up. That's for certain, but I love him. Know what Shiz Ota said to me? 'We're all refugees of one thing or another.' I guess we've all been hurt, we've all been displaced. We're the walking wounded."

"Sometimes I get so discouraged," Ruth said.

"Ruth, don't let Freddy get away just because he's a damned fool man with no more sense of direction than a piss ant."

Ruth didn't know if she was laughing or crying in Caroline's arms. She and Caroline and Clarinet, all wrapped up together in the big chair by the fire.

In mid-February Louie Riccetti and his nephew Tony went back to Washington D.C. to receive the award for the Nation's best corn grower. The DELTA HERALD published a long article about it. Ruth wrote it herself. And she got Charlene to take the photograph that accompanied the newspaper article, a portrait of Louie in his coat and tie sitting at Ruth's kitchen table. Charlene was also the town photographer. She had a German camera with two different lenses.

Elsie Phipps, the postmistress, was thrilled to read the post card postmarked Washington D.C. and addressed to Ruth:

Good Trip. See you soon.

Louie

Two weeks before the Music Festival and the State Band Competition it started to rain. Rain in February was normal, and the storms were strong enough to blow the tule fog out of the valley. Everybody's spirits picked up. There was a real sense of anticipation about the Music Festival and the State Competition, too. Even Ruth was feeling hopeful. Maybe, she thought, Caroline was right about Freddy. Maybe he just needed some encouragement. She closed the door to her office and picked up the telephone. On the other hand, maybe she would spook him. Maybe he'd run like a scared jackrabbit if she made any move in his direction. She was thirty-four years old, for heaven's sake. She ought to be able to make a telephone call to a man without getting butterflies in her belly.

Nettie at the telephone company came on the line," That you Ruth? Anything wrong?"

"No, Nettie," said Ruth. "Only the usual turmoil around here. I'm doing six things at once. I didn't realize I'd had the receiver off the hook so long."

"Just checking," said Nettie.

Ruth put down the receiver. "Damn it all," she said to herself, "goldfish mate in fishbowls." She picked up the phone again and dialed Freddy's number at the pharmacy.

"Freddy Noble," she said, a little abruptly, "the Friday after the State Band Competition I'm inviting you to dinner in Sacramento."

"A celebration?" asked Freddy.

"Win, lose or draw," said Ruth. "I figure I owe you one for those beautiful uniforms." She laughed softly, "You've strengthened my brass section considerably, too."

"You don't owe me a thing, Ruth, but I'd like to have dinner with you. I'll make the reservation."

"No," she started to say, "this is my party," then she checked herself. "Oh, let me do this," she said.

"I might be forced to reciprocate," said Freddy.

"Up to you," said Ruth.

She hung up the phone and realized that she was blushing from head to toe. Partly it was the hunch that everybody in Two Sloughs would know the contents of the phone call before lunch time. Partly it was because she'd left herself wide open for the first time in a long time, and if she'd been standing in her office stark naked, she couldn't have felt more vulnerable.

Ruth picked up the phone once more and called Ursula Brown, the District Psychologist. "Ursula, I'm looking for a nice, quiet restaurant in Sacramento, with good food."

"Romantic setting?" asked Ursula.

"No," snapped Ruth. Then she laughed, "Ursula, why don't you go get yourself a crystal ball and take up fortune telling full time. This school psychology stuff doesn't do justice to your true talents."

"Actually, school psychology is just fortune telling without the colorful head scarf and the dangly earrings."

"O.K.," said Ruth, "good food, romantic setting."

"Emilio's. I take it you're not inviting me to come along," said Ursula.

"Afraid not," said Ruth.

Folks in town chatted about the band costumes and the hats, leaning on the meat counter at Ping Lowe's Market. People laughed about the sets for the school Music Festival with the tellers at the Bank of Thurgood Bream. Everybody talked about the State Band Competition. This was the year Two Sloughs was going to take first prize.

Mrs. Weaver kept the crowd at Ike's up to date on the costumes as she washed up. The walls at Ike's were imperceptibly changing color, as if the tule fog was lifting day by day. And the linoleum was developing a pattern that no one knew it had. Not that the men ever talked to Mrs. Weaver. At first they had tried to make awkward conversation, but her head shot up, and her jawbone jutted out, and everything she said seemed to end with an unspoken, "You wanna make somethin' of it?" They gave it up. Now she came in the afternoon, and Ike got the news as he and Mrs. Weaver cleaned up. The next morning he would pass it along. "Mrs. Weaver says that Shiz Ota's a magician with a pair of scissors. She cut down a jacket to fit that little Nakamura boy, no bigger than a jackrabbit.... Mrs. Weaver's kids claim Lionel's getting to be hot stuff with that trombone of his." Ike always called her Mrs. Weaver.

Mrs. Weaver became friendly with Ike's wife Emma, too. Emma had always refused help around the house. Her pride wouldn't let her admit she couldn't do it. But Ike explained how it was with Mrs. Weaver, how badly she needed the work. Emma saw how Mrs. Weaver had more pride than she had, how she wouldn't take charity, those skinny arms of hers sticking out of a sweater all shrunk and darned and two sizes too small, barely holding together. Well, Emma knew she'd met her match when it came to pride.

She'd just have to ask Mrs. Weaver for help or Mrs. Weaver wouldn't accept the sweaters Emma had already started knitting for the children or the dresses Emma had grown too fat for.

Emma knew she would have to confess to Mrs. Weaver that there were some things she didn't like to ask Ike to do, personal things, taking off her braces to shave her legs, scrubbing the bathroom floor when she had an accident.

"Would it bother you to help me with my bath?" Emma asked her one day.

Mrs. Weaver straightened up and looked Emma in the eye. "No," she said.

"The thing is my legs are pretty disgusting, kind of shriveled, but the braces are a pain in the neck to get off, and I hate for Ike to have to help me. It's so...." Emma blushed.

Mrs. Weaver hadn't taken her eyes off Emma's face. "Must be tough," she said.

"Well, if you wouldn't mind it...." Emma said.

"Where do we start?" asked Mrs. Weaver.

Both women began to relax their guard. Ike watched in amazement as Mrs. Weaver's clenched-teeth tightness began to melt away in Emma's benign presence. And Emma's taut, tired, brave face, which had caused Ike so much worry lately, began to soften, too. She wasn't trying to do quite so much. She began to look younger. Ike came home early one day and caught Emma knitting while Mrs. Weaver scrubbed the floor around her wheelchair on hands and knees. They were talking over the town gossip, chattering like sparrows, discussing the Weaver children, who all began to acquire heavy navy blue wool sweaters and matching socks. The girls had knee socks to match their red and blue plaid skirts. Nobody but Emma and Shiz Ota and Mrs. Weaver knew that they had been the St. Ignatius school uniforms thirty-five years ago. Emma had always said they might come in handy.

Ike knew it was some sort of miracle, but it was a woman's miracle. He knew enough to stay the hell out of it. His Emma was more like her old self again. And if Ike's Cafe smelled too much like Lysol, so what?

One afternoon Lionel lagged behind after band practice. Ruth was suspicious. She didn't like to leave him alone in the auditorium with all the sets.

"You need something, Lionel?

The tails of his flannel shirt had come untucked, and his pant cuffs were splattered with mud.

"I can't get it." He spoke to the varnished floor, chin down.

"What?"

"I can't get the cadenza." He scratched at the scab on his nose. "It's too hard." He looked up at her suddenly, accusingly, but tears lurked right behind the glare. He sniffled and wiped his nose on his sleeve. This was a cry for help, and Ruth knew it.

"Yes," she said slowly. She put down her stack of sheet music. "Yes, it is hard. I wouldn't even have brought it up except that you're such a natural musician -- good sense of rhythm, round tone...."

"My Dad says I'm not trying," Lionel interrupted. "But I am." His voice cracked.

"Well, let's look at the darned thing." She picked Tommy Randolph's trumpet out of his trumpet case and sat down in Tommy's chair, next to Lionel's. "Sit," she said. "I can't play trumpet worth beans, so don't pay any attention to me. I'm just here for the timing. Let's try the first three measures, real slow, like a funeral march." She tapped a slow beat with her foot.

She really was a terrible trumpet player. She made Lionel laugh and lose his lip. "Sorry," she said, "I warned you I was awful. Let's try it again."

They worked on the cadenza for about an hour, measure by measure. Ruth knew she had promised Mrs. McClatchy that she would help her collate a Gold Rush booklet for the fifth grade, but Lionel had asked for help. Suddenly this seemed like the most important thing in the world, the two of them sitting together side by side working through the cadenza, figuring out the phrasing, where Lionel could breathe, giggling over Ruth's squawks and sputters.

"Beautiful, Lionel," Ruth said when they finally had put it all together. She chuckled, "Actually, the trumpet stank, but you played beautifully. You know, I think I like that cadenza a little slower anyway."

"It's sure easier."

"Yeah, but it kind of makes it stand out more at that tempo. I think I was rushing it."

"Thanks."

"You're welcome." She put her hand on his shoulder, and to her amazement he didn't flinch. He sat with her hand resting lightly on his shoulder and looked down at his trombone. She watched him swallow hard. "You tell your Dad for me that you are, too, trying," she said gently. "And you're doing well."

He squirmed in his chair. She let her hand fall and winked at him, "Do me a favor, though. Don't tell your Dad about the terrible trumpet."

Lionel laughed, a high-pitched, little boy laugh, packed up his trombone and went home. Ruth watched him disappear out the door lugging his trombone case with both hands, listing a little to the left to compensate for the bulky weight of it. What went on in the heads of eleven-year-old boys? They seemed to her the most rough-cut and at the same time the most fragile of her students. At eleven the girls already possessed a sort of civilized saviness. They were shaped. Little Women. The boys, on the other hand, broke out of babyhood at a run, savages, refusing to be caught or gentled or tamed into manhood. Then when you'd given up on them, turned your back on them, they came up and nuzzled you from behind.

Ruth knew this was her big chance at the State Band Competition. Barbara Kramer was back in first chair, first clarinet. Suzanne Weaver was first saxophone. With those trombone and trumpet cadenzas tucked into the Sousa marches, they had as good a chance as they would ever have to carry off first prize. Somehow it seemed more important this year. Freddy's and Shiz's uniforms, Tommy Randolph's solos, Lionel's cadenzas -- there seemed to be more riding on this one.

Ruth was so intent on whipping the band and the chorus into shape, she scarcely noticed when a new storm swept in, a warm storm. It rained up to an elevation of 7000 feet in the Sierra. Ten days straight it rained.

The men patrolled the levees twenty-four hours a day now, in shifts, looking for potholes, seeps, boils, forming work crews to sandbag. The land inside the islands was all below sea level, and this time of year, with the river rising every day, it was way below river level, subject to flooding. Only the man-made levees kept the Sacramento Delta from becoming a vast inland sea in winter. The men understood how tenuous their hold was on the islands that were their homes, how puny their levees looked in the face of the torrent of water that gushed out of the Sierra.

The town of Two Sloughs was actually situated on two islands. The businesses, the school, Japan Town, Ike's Cafe were all on Bream Island on the east side of the Sacramento River. The "white section" of town, the Catholic and Presbyterian churches were on Lambert Island on the west side of the river. The Two Sloughs Drawbridge connected the two islands. Beaver Slough and Steamboat Slough branched off just south of the bridge, forming yet another island. A series of islands surrounded by levees formed a fragile patchwork that stretched fifty miles in every direction to the verge of San Francisco Bay. A thousand miles of levee strained against the forces of the water. A thousand miles of levee had to be watched.

Every morning when the men stopped at Ike's to check in, some of them just going off patrol, soaked to the skin, smelling of wet wool and tobacco, some of them just going on, they eyed the height of the river against the pilings that supported the back end of Ike's Cafe. Relentlessly, day after day, the water rose.

Barbara Kramer was back in the clarinet section. Her broken arm was healed, but she was rusty. She needed about two weeks of straight practice, and Ruth had three days. Ruth had scheduled the School Music Festival for February 22, one week before the State Band Competition. The Wednesday before the Music Festival, Ruth sat in her office trying to figure out how she could bargain with Mrs. Miyasaki for one more practice on Thursday, which was a Japanese School afternoon.

Elsie Phipps called from the Post Office just before noon. "They're issuing flood warnings for our side of the river, Ruth. I guess you'd better send everybody across the bridge."

"But we've got a band re...." Ruth felt ashamed of herself. Flood warnings were serious. There were procedures to be followed. She could see mothers driving up in front of the school right now. She rang the fire drill bell and started down the hall to tell the teachers.

Within an hour, the school was empty. Two Sloughs mothers didn't quibble about whose child was whose. They filled their cars and station wagons with as many kids as they could hold, took them across the river to the Catholic Church, then came back for more. They gathered up all the kids whose mothers didn't have cars and the children who lived farthest away. They manned the telephone in Ruth's office and reassured frantic mothers who called. As the last children were being sorted out, one of the mothers stuck her head out into the hall.

"Ruth, It's Freddy. Says he needs to talk to you. Says it's important."

Ruth picked up the phone, "Hi, Freddy. Lionel's already over at the church."

"I wanted to be sure you were getting out, Ruth. Really. Don't stick around worrying about the building or anything."

"We're on our way."

"Do you want me to come over?"

"No, we're fine. We're headed for the church right now."

"Be careful. These levees are water-logged. No telling what they'll do."

"O.K., Fred." The mothers were milling around her desk waiting for instructions.

"I just don't want anything to happen...."

"Freddy...." The mothers looked up expectantly. "Freddy.... I'll see you later. I've got to get these mothers out of here," she said a shade too desperately.

She had dispatched the last mothers when the phone rang again. It was the sheriff. "We're loading up the last kids, Carl. We'll be out of here in about ten minutes," she said.

"I knew you'd have it under control. We've got a high tide due in about three hours, so we're running out of time on your side of the river. I've got a favor to ask you, Ruth."

"Sure, Carl, shoot."

"The levee behind Japan Town is giving us the most trouble. I put a crew on it early this morning, but they've disappeared. Tosh says Old Man Bream came by and pulled them off."

"How could he do that?" Ruth asked.

"He's probably got 'em sandbagging the Bank. Figures that's worth more than all Japan Town put together. But why he'd leave the school unprotected...."

"Yeah, why," said Ruth grimly.

"Well, we've got to move those people out. If that back levee on Bream Island goes, it'll take Japan Town out as well as the school. We've got to get them over the bridge to Lambert Island, just in case.

"Oh, my God."

"Anyway, some horse's ass of a Red Cross worker showed up in Japan Town about an hour ago and uttered the word 'evacuation.' There's mass hysteria over there. Last time they heard the word 'evacuation' was World War II. All they can think of is those damned concentration camps. I'm up in Sacramento. My deputy's in Elk Grove. We've got a hell of a mess over there. I called Doc Graham, and he said he'd get over there as soon as he could, but you're closest. I thought maybe you could...."

"Right. I'll go straight over."

"Thanks, Ruth. I'll get down soon as I can."

She hung up and dialed Elsie at the Post Office. "Elsie, can you meet me in Japan Town? Some fool said the word 'evacuation' over there, and all hell's broken loose." She gave last instructions to Mr. Mundorf to turn off the gas and the electricity, grabbed her raincoat and drove over to the Buddhist Temple, a block away. She'd guessed right.

The crowd around the temple shouted, shoved to get into the tiny temple. The old women stood out in the rain bare-headed, without raincoats, wailing. Ruth spotted Tosh Nakamura. She waded through the old ladies, who clung to her and cried. "What do you want me to do, Tosh?"

"Get rid of those Red Cross workers."

They were easy to spot. Three white faces in identical blue raincoats. They carried clipboards and stood utterly dazed by the havoc they'd wrought. "This way, gentlemen. Follow me," Ruth said in her most authoritarian, school principal voice. She turned sharply away and marched toward her car, hoping she could get them into it before she had to explain. Her gamble worked. The stupefied young men followed obediently, and Elsie drove up at that moment. Ruth shoved the three Red Cross workers into the back of Elsie's car. "Explain to them what the word 'evacuation' means around here, would you -- a brief history of the Second World War, that sort of thing. Take them over to the Presbyterian Church." She slammed the car door.

"Don't you mean the Catholic Church?" asked Elsie.

"No. Definitely not. The Presbyterian Church. Tell them over there that we need more cars."

Elsie laughed and drove off. Things were already calming down around Tosh Nakamura. Ruth began organizing cars while Tosh worked at removing the altarpieces from the Buddhist Church. She lined up all the available cars and trucks behind Tosh's car, which held the incense burners, the candlesticks and Reverend Miyasaki. The Buddhist priest sat calmly staring straight ahead in the front seat holding the gold Buddha nestled inside the hollow bell. As soon as the old ladies saw the priest and the altarpieces in the first car, they filed into the cars behind it. More cars were already arriving from across the river. Many of the children from Japan Town had walked home from school instead of getting into cars and going across the river. Ruth should have thought of that and kept an eye on them. But the children were used to following orders from Ruth. "Fumiko," she said, "put the younger ones on your laps. You older kids hold the little ones. You're only going across the river to Lambert Island, so crowd in." Some of the children were missing because they had gotten in the car pools at school and gone over to the church. The mothers were frantic. She sent four of the eighth grade boys she knew she could trust door to door. "Be sure nobody is left behind," she said. "Each of you take a street. Toshi," Ruth said in a loud voice, "run inside your house and call Dr. Graham's office. Tell him to meet you at the Catholic Church." Then she assured the mothers that Dr. Graham would be waiting for them at the church across the river with pills for the grandmothers. Doc had told her one time that the grandmothers put great faith in pills. Caroline Graham drove by with Shiz Ota and a carload of white uniforms. They both waved.

Had Bream, with no authority whatsoever, really pulled a crew off the back levee to save his miserable bank? How had he gotten away with it? But even as she asked herself the question, she could imagine him stomping out to that back levee, testily ordering the crew to a new site, ordering them to hurry up about it. Heck, the crew boss probably thought he was the governor. Was Bream so vindictive that he would destroy Japan Town and risk the lives of all the children in Two Sloughs simply to get even with her?

She shuddered. She was imagining things. The old coot was beginning to get under her skin. Besides in the ten years Ruth had been at the school, their levees had never broken. The men kept too close an eye on them. The river got high every couple of years, and islands around them flooded, but the levees on their two islands had held. The county was merely taking precautions. Carl wasn't an alarmist, though. And he was the sheriff. She had to take him seriously, even if Old Man Bream didn't.

The four eighth grade boys came back, leading Mrs. Kobayashi and a gunnysack full of leeks. "She wouldn't leave without them," they said. The boys declared the blocks of Japan Town empty. They piled in the last car with Elsie, who had made a second trip. Ruth drove back to the school. She'd better make one last check, just in case.

Mr. Mundorf had already locked up and left. She let herself in, flipped the light switch in the hall and then remembered the electricity had been turned off. The sky was so black that the building was nearly dark. The rain spattered against the windows. She went into her office in the gloom, picked up her purse, and her attendance record, and then she remembered the band instruments. They had practiced this morning on the auditorium floor while Mr. Mundorf did some last minute work on the sets up on the stage. She had told the band to leave their instruments beside their chairs. She hurried down the hall. If she moved them up onto the stage they would be much safer from high water. The auditorium had terrible drainage. Down on the floor they would be ruined by even minor flooding.

When she opened the auditorium door she was startled by the darkness of the room. There were no windows in the auditorium. She should have realized that. The rain pounded on the high roof of the auditorium drowning out her footsteps as she rushed around collecting clarinets and flutes, tripping over music stands in the dark, hefting the trombones and the tuba, pushing them all well back on the stage. She really should put them up on the boat, but she had to get over to the Catholic Church. Poor Father Giulio didn't know the whole of Japan Town was on its way to his church, lugging their Buddhist altarpieces along with them. What time was it? She went out into the hall and looked at her watch. They were already there, in fact. She was almost an hour behind them. She had better get going. She went back down the dim hall to her office, tried to think of what she should take, then decided she was being silly. She locked the front door and walked out to her car in the pouring rain.

The noise of the river was the first thing that alerted her to danger. A licking, lapping sound. Closer, not particularly loud or menacing, but closer. She looked toward Japan Town, but her glasses were streaked with rain. She splashed through the puddles to her car, got in, took her glasses off, and was looking for a handkerchief in her purse when she felt the car rock slightly. She dropped her purse, put her key in the ignition and started her car. She'd better get out of here. The engine fired right up, she started to back out, looking over her inside shoulder the way her Dad had taught her, then shifted into first. The engine died. The car bobbled, half afloat. "Damn," she said, "the levee's gone," and she turned the key again, then again.

The water was coming in over the floorboards now. When she opened the car door, she could see it moving past her with some speed. She'd better make a run for the school steps. She got out, but with her glasses off she misjudged the force of the water. Half way to the school steps she stepped in a hole. The water swept her off her feet. She splashed around on her hands and knees, half crawling, half swimming, fighting to keep her head up, but she couldn't get her footing until she was carried past the flag pole. She grabbed at the pole and hung on while she righted herself, coughing, gasping for breath.

There was no use trying to get back to the school steps. The current was too strong. The water flooded past her filling the island like a huge dirty bathtub. It was above her knees now. She'd lost her high-heeled shoes. She edged around the base of the flagpole. "O.K." she said, "here goes," and lunged for one of the three redwood trees the class of 1907 had planted to commemorate Luther Burbank's visit to the school. The cold of the water numbed her legs. The current sucked her feet out from under her. Her hands stung. She caught a lower branch on the nearest tree and worked her way in to the trunk, fighting to keep footing in the current, struggling to catch her breath. She hitched her skirt up around her waist, grabbed on to the prickly branches above her and hauled herself up out of the water onto a lower branch. "Ouch!" she yelped. She balanced there, clinging to a higher branch, shivering, pushing her hair back out of her eyes.

The water was gaining on her. She had to get higher before her hands got too numb to hang on. "All right now, watch it," she scolded herself, as if she were some slow second grader. "Take it one at a t-t-time." Her teeth were chattering. She knew the tree was climbable. She'd yelled at the boys a hundred times to get down out of this tree. She began to labor slowly up the wet, slippery limbs, muttering to herself when she lost her footing. Who made redwoods so prickly? She climbed clumsily, teetering on the slick tree limbs in her stocking feet, scraping her forearms on the rough bark of the trunk as she pulled herself up. For some crazy reason, Caroline Graham's words kept whirling around in her head. "So who hasn't danced on a table once in his life?"

If only the rain would stop so she could see something. Finally she worked her way up to a place where the redwood tree had been vandalized years ago and had sent up a second trunk; and in the cleft between the two trunks she managed to wedge herself into a V filled with old redwood branches. Holding on to the branch beside her she was able to sit straddling the notch, with her back against the main trunk. She looked out through the branches at the school. Her car was almost completely submerged. The water was rising up the steps of the school. She couldn't see without her glasses whether the water was up to the door. If only she had been able to get to the school building. She should have tried again before the water got so high. It had happened so fast, that she had still doubted the levee break, still disbelieved the flood, even while it washed her past the front steps. Between her and the school building half a shed roof swept past, trailing a power line and a screen door in its wake. It disappeared before Ruth could identify where it had come from. A patch of peat dirt ten feet across floated by with dead grasses on it and a willow bush, moving very fast, twirling slightly in the flow. Freddy had warned her that peat dirt would do that -- saturate with water and just float away, leaving a gaping hole in the levee for the water to rush into. The levee must have broken on the back side of the island for it to have happened so fast, and the cross check behind the school must have given way, too. There was no chance of getting over to the school buildings now. And it wouldn't do any good. Lord, the water was half way up the school windows already. She wiped her eyes. She wished she hadn't lost her glasses. She wished she could see better.

The men had joined the county crew sandbagging the bank and the store, the half dozen businesses up on the levee: Ike's, the pharmacy, when the deputy sheriff ordered them to the other side of the bridge. "You've done all you can. I don't like the look of that back levee. There was supposed to be a crew back there.... I want everybody off Bream Island. Get over the bridge. Get a move on."

The deputy pounded on the door of the Bream's apartment above the bank. Alexander Bream cracked a window, "I'm not leaving."

"Look, Mr. Bream. I got orders. This is martial law around here now."

"Then you better come up and shoot me. I'm not going."

The deputy turned to the men, "God Almighty. What do I do now?" he asked.

"Be a waste of a good bullet to shoot him," said Harvey. "We all heard you warn him," said Dan.

"You got more important things," said Freddy. Freddy had thrown on his slicker and his irrigating boots and joined the men as soon as the deputy had evacuated the pharmacy. "Is everybody else cleared out?" asked Louie.

"Yeah. Checked the school. All locked up."

"Seen Ruth?" asked Freddy.

"She was over in Japan Town loading up the last of the old ladies." The deputy chuckled. "She was promising them pills if they hurried up. That was over an hour ago. Everybody's out."

"Maybe I better go back inside and get some vitamin pills to pass out," Freddy said.

"No," said the deputy. "I got a bad feeling about that back levee. High tide'll be due any minute now. Get out of here." He turned to the county crew, "You guys are slow as mud," he said. "Go on. Git."

Ping Lowe was the last one over the drawbridge. He and his wife had loaded their car with groceries of their store shelves until the car nearly sagged. The deputy sheriff waved them through, and they headed for the Catholic church. Mrs. Lowe's lap was full of cabbages.

The men moved over to the Lambert Island side of the bridge and began sandbagging the west anchorage. Freddy borrowed a shovel from Louie and went to work. The men were soaked clear through now, with rain and sweat. The rain kept falling like a punishment on them, almost business-like, dripping off their hats, down the backs of their necks, as if it were in partnership with the river and never meant to quit 'til they were washed away for good.

So they were working on the Lambert Island levee across the river from Ike's and the pharmacy and the bank and the school when they saw the water coming. Dan Martin was up in the back of his flat-bed truck unloading empty sandbags and happened to look up. As if a flood gate had opened, the water swept through a break in the back levee and across Bream Island on the opposite side of the river, toward Japan Town, toward the school, toward the near levee that held the bank, the grocery store, the pharmacy. Right toward Ike's.

"Look out!" Dan Martin hollered. Jesus, it's comin' fast. Look out!"

Ben jumped up into the bed of the truck, "Shoot, it'll break out this side and come straight for us," Ben said.

"Christ Almighty!"

The two men leapt off the truck, but there was no place to go. The water surged across Bream Island on the other side of the river from where they stood, headed directly at them. They all knew that when a levee broke, the force of the water usually caused a levee break on the opposite side of the island, where the wave of water first hit the opposite levee head on.   They all knew that the broken levee could easily surge across the main channel and dash against the levee of Lambert Island, which was where they stood, a domino effect, wiping out the levee they stood on, the levee that protected all the school children, all the population of Japan Town, holed up in the Catholic church, the levee that surrounded their homes and their wives, who were so busy organizing spaghetti dinners and blankets that they weren't even paying attention. The men all climbed back up onto the bed of Dan's truck and watched the water batter Japan Town. The water headed toward the levee right above the Two Sloughs Drawbridge. It headed smack at Ike's Cafe. Unconsciously they closed ranks, stood close together in a line with their hands in their jacket pockets, feet spread slightly apart, facing the river.

They saw the wave smash up against the levee under Ike's Cafe, saw the structure stagger as if it had received a low punch, right itself, then lurch as the levee beneath the building sustained the brunt of the water's force. They saw a cottonwood tree next to Ike's go over and a crack in the levee begin to widen, crumpling in on itself. They watched the sandbags they had filled begin to topple into the river. Puny they looked now, pathetically undersized.

But the crippled cafe clung to the levee some way. Its spindly back legs, planted out in the river, held. The break began to gush water directly beneath Ike's. Still the old shack clutched at the levee bank, stubborn, stupid to the forces that threatened it. A second wave of water hit the break, and now a torrent of water rushed between the pilings of the old shack. The cafe stumbled, the thin legs broke, one after another, and slowly Ike's Cafe slid over on its side and pitched into the river, smashing against the pilings of the Two Sloughs Bridge, breaking in two as it swept under the bridge at a cockeyed angle, then around the bend in the river. A window frame spit up by the current caught a last glint of light and reflected it back at the men.

No one spoke. They still stood in a line, shoulder to shoulder, heads turned downstream to follow the shack around the bend of the river. Ike's Cafe had deflected the wave, probably saved the island they stood on, possibly saved their lives, their families' lives. They knew with sick certainty that the loss of Bream Island across the river had relieved the pressure of the floodwaters on their own Lambert Island and probably saved their homes.

The bitter aftertaste of their good fortune was nothing new to them. In farming, one district's crop failure often meant a "good year" for some other region. But it was hard to celebrate a victory in the face of such enormous loss. Had the levee behind Japan Town been as well patrolled as their own? Had those farmers had the resources to fight the flood: the trucks full of hay bales, the sandbags, the manpower? What happened to the crew the deputy had talked about?

"Son of a bitch, we owe Ike one," said Louie finally. "Who'd a thought that old shack would put up such a hell of a fight?"

"I hope they got everybody out over there. It looks like a god damned inland sea."

"I hope Ruth's O.K." Freddy said. "Anybody see her cross the bridge?"

Nobody said a word. Freddy didn't even realize he'd given himself away. Nobody called him on it. They let it go.

Ruth shifted her position slightly and peered out into the dusk. A vast dark lake surrounded her, edged by a smudge of trees that marked the levee of the island. The water had quieted down. The levee break must have reached a kind of equilibrium with the river. But the water beneath her must be ten or twelve feet deep. Her car was completely submerged. Only the rooftop of the school poked out of the muddy water. She thought of Mr. Mundorf's beautiful blue cardboard boat with its yard of sails trapped in the flooded auditorium, the drowned instruments, the mimeograph machine. Her school was ruined. The water had risen up to about six feet below her perch now. Had she climbed high enough in the redwood tree? "Here's to Luther Burbank," she thought. That was the song the school sang every year on Luther Burbank's birthday as they planted another tree in his honor. Was the water still rising? The high tide should have come by now. What time was it? It was nearly dark. 5:30? 6:00? How long could she hold out here? Soaking wet, and in this weather. Her hands were already so numb she could barely hang onto the branches. Somebody would come look for her before too long. Who? Who would notice she was missing? With school closed, would anybody notice she was gone? A sad, hollow lump began to form inside her, an ache. Who cared?

"I just don't want anything to happen to you," Freddy had said, well, started to say. She'd stopped him. Oh, Freddy....

She shook herself. Clarinet cared. She'd be yowling her head off. Mice for dinner tonight, Missy. Well, Ruth Hardy, you got yourself into this. You had better get yourself out. You're the independent one. Remember? "Here's to Luther Burbank," the song kept running through her head. She was shivering. She'd better do something about that. She buttoned up her raincoat and pressed as much water out of her wool sweater and skirt as she could. She wrung out her wool scarf and tied it over her head. She found a pair of gloves and a plastic rain hood in her inside raincoat pocket. She put the plastic rain hood over her wool scarf, pulled on the wet wool gloves and put her hands in her pockets. At the bottom of one pocket she felt an old package of Lifesavers stuck to the lining of her raincoat. She pulled them out and sucked one -- cherry. She put the rest back in her pocket. Oh, boy, she was cold.

"Here's to Luther Burbank, wizard of the flowers,
Came to Santa Rosa and worked for hours and hours...."

One of the fourth graders had written that song. With her back against the trunk she was out of the wind, at least, and the rain seemed to have stopped. She couldn't tell if the water was still rising. Oh, God, it was definitely dark now. The chances of anybody looking for her after dark were nil. She was in for a long, cold night, and it was her own darned fault. She could hear the gang at Ike's discussing her,

"Carl said he called her himself and told her. Said he warned her about the high tide at 3:00."

"Elsie said she was right behind her when they left Japan Town."

Was Ike's still there? It was up on the levee. Was Freddy's Pharmacy gone? They were up on the levee. They should be all right. Wet maybe, but all right. Only the school and Japan Town were down off the levee, completely flooded. She'd read of rats clinging to flotsam in a flood. Would they climb into trees?

"I just don't want anything to happen to you," Freddy had said. Would Freddy look for her?

"No more sense of direction than a piss ant," Caroline had said. She wished Freddy would look for her. She was scared.

"Bred a thornless cactus," she sang, "an almond with a prune,
Thirty thousand prune trees, grafted off by June.
Here's to Luther Burbank..."

She was so very scared.

Charlene was helping Shiz Ota set up a makeshift Buddhist shrine in the Catholic Social Hall. It had been Charlene's idea. "You can't set Buddha in a corner with the broom and the dustpan," she told Father Giulio. "Anyway, we need all the help we can get in the prayer department."

Father Giulio had a soft spot for Charlene. He had married Charlene and Larry ten years before, and he'd heard Charlene's confessions ever since. He dug up an old altar cloth, which the women draped over a wheeled serving cart.

"Heck," said Charlene, "we've got a Book Mobile and a Blood Mobile. Why not a Buddha Mobile?"

Shiz delighted in Charlene's bountiful arrangement of fruit on the rolling altar. "The Buddhists could use you, Charlene. You have a real flair."

"Father Giulio's pretty strict about his altar. I never get to go all out," Charlene said, gesturing with her hands. "You know what I mean? Let's light the incense. All you can smell around here is spaghetti sauce."

The women of Japan Town worked elbow to elbow with the women of Lambent Tract, cutting up coleslaw, chopping Mrs. Kobayashi's leeks, making spaghetti sauce, sleeves pushed up, dishtowels tied around their waists. They all knew that Japan Town was probably underwater by now, everything lost. Again. They would have to start over. Again. And yet a kind of euphoria filled the hot steamy kitchen of the Catholic Social Hall. Everybody was safe, together. For the first time anybody in Two Sloughs could remember, everybody worked together. Mrs. Lowe opened cans of tomatoes from the cases she and Ping had brought. Tosh organized a patrol to relieve the men on the levee watch. Another group of men from Japan Town were out helping Father Giulio clear the downspouts and the gutters of the Catholic Church.

All the women were in the kitchen patching together a dinner from everybody's can cupboards and Ping Lowe's grocery. Mrs. Weaver and Mrs. Matsubara were cleaning the bathrooms. Retta Mae and Emma had found a basket of toys somewhere and were entertaining the youngest children in the back hall.

When the Red Cross called from Sacramento, old Grandma Scoleri took the call because she knew where the telephone was, "Hello! Hello? What?.............. We got a lot of foreigners around here," she hollered into the receiver.

Caroline Graham glided up, "Thank you Mrs. Scoleri, aaahl take that," she said smoothly.

"Caroline uses that southern drawl like a cleaver," Charlene muttered in admiration.

"This is Mrs. Graham, Doctor Graham's wife," Caroline became quite business-like. "Thank you," she said, "but we're quite well organized down here. Ping Lowe's Grocery donated the food. A few extra blankets is all we need, when you get the chance. We take care of our own in Two Sloughs." Tears pooled in the eyes of the women of Japan Town and the women of Lambert Tract as they listened to her, but they were all chopping onions. It could have been the onions.

It was well after dark, as the women were dishing up dinner at the Catholic Church, when somebody noticed Ruth's chicken and barley soup was missing. Good night for it. The rain had stopped, but a sharp north wind blew.

"Charlene, have you heard from Ruth? I hope she's bringing her soup," Caroline asked.

"She'll be along. She stayed at school 'til the last minute. She probably didn't get to it 'til late."

By 7:00 o'clock Ruth still hadn't shown up. Elsie said she'd left Japan Town when Elsie did. "She was just going over to check the school one last time. But that was early. Maybe 3:30."

Charlene didn't say any more, but when her husband came by she pulled him aside. "Honey, I'm up to my eyeballs in spaghetti sauce. Do me a favor. Go down and check on Ruth."

"Christ, Charlene, Ruth's all right."

"Larry, just do it, O.K.? I'm asking as a favor. I just got this funny feeling."

Larry's eyes rolled, "You and your funny feelings. All right! All right! What the hell. She could probably use help with her soup pot."

But when Larry got down to the Giannini ranch, Ruth's house was dark. The cat was at the front door straggly wet and mad. Larry went inside, found some cat food in the refrigerator, fed the cat, looked around. Ruth hadn't been there since breakfast. Her cereal bowl was soaking in the sink. "Charlene and her god-damned funny feelings," he muttered.

He wasn't worried about Ruth, really. The woman had a good head on her shoulders. She wasn't the kind to go get herself in trouble. On the other hand, it was his experience that you couldn't always predict what a woman would do. A man now, he could see trouble coming a mile off. But a woman. There seemed to be no telling with a woman. It was like they all had loose steering. They're going along straight and fine. Next thing you know they've veered off.... He was thinking about Charlene now and her "funny feeling" and her "deep sinks" and her rages. He tried to read Charlene's moods by the kind of nightgown she put on every night -- her flannel nightgown with the high neck all buttoned up, her old raggedy cotton shift. Sometimes she'd get into bed with nothing on at all under that ratty wool robe of hers.

But Ruth was, well, more dependable, more like a man. Still he'd better mention it to the sheriff.

Ruth listened, but she couldn't hear whether the floodwater was rising. The water rushed by secretly, under the cover of the darkness. Occasionally it would slap against the trunk of her redwood tree, a sodden, ominous sound.

Here's to Luther Burbank."

And it sounded closer, very close.

Sometimes she would think she could see it glinting right beneath her feet, but it was pitch dark now. She could barely make out the branch she clung to. She was afraid she would doze and slip off her straddled perch. "Don't give Bream the satisfaction," she said to herself. Holding on to the branch above her, she gingerly shifted her legs a little to get some circulation going. She rubbed her thighs with her one free hand.

"Well, Ruth," her mother would have said if she were still alive, "you always said you wanted a challenge." Her bony, ambitious mother, with her icy eyes and a chin that meant business. Pushing, pushing. "Get a career. Look after yourself. Don't get stuck like I did." "Stuck" meant a husband who was a car salesman, who never quite made his draw. "Stuck" meant two babies before she turned twenty-two. "Stuck" meant teaching piano lessons in the living room to everybody else's children to make ends meet. "Stuck" meant getting yourself into the crotch of a redwood tree with no way out. "Poor Ruthie," her father would have said. Her father had been a round, cheery man who loved his girls, indulged them with picnics on the riverbank and fishing trips in the back sloughs. Ruth would have said she'd had a happy childhood if it hadn't been for her mother's bitten, disappointed lower lip and her father's helpless, watery eyes.

A heavy splash broke her reverie, soaked her, a thunderous crashing sound beside her in the dark. A wave rocked her redwood tree, and it trembled. She clutched her branch. The redwood tree beside her had fallen over, its roots dislodged by the floodwaters. Oh, God, how long before her tree went over too? Were redwood trees shallow rooted or deep rooted? She couldn't remember. What could she do? Could she jump free once it started to fall? Should she get down now and try to swim for the school roof? In the dark? Could she even climb the steep pitch of the roof if she managed to get to it?

This was the kind of jam that her sister used to get into. Ruth was always stuck with figuring how to get her out. Her thin, brittle, beautiful sister, who looked ready to crack to pieces. She thought of Jeanie at her kitchen table in Oregon, that raggedy nightgown, crying.

"I told you, Jeanie, that someday you'd have to rescue me," Ruth said. Then she thought of Jeanie at her kitchen table, too distracted to notice, too overwhelmed to help.

"Well, Ruth," her mother would have said, "you got yourself into this. You'd better get yourself out of it. Nobody on God's green earth is going to help you."

She was shivering badly. Oh, Freddy, help.

About eight o'clock Mr. Yee turned up from the China Camp whorehouse with a car load of canned goods from his sister's store and four smooth, round, luscious young women wearing rubber gloves. "No English," he said, "but they wash dishes real good. Sorry we late. We go up two towns before we find a bridge to cross river. Where Harold and Roland?"

Retta Mae threw her arms around the four women and led them to the sinks, telling them their skin was much too beautiful to be in the dish pans, but they were wonderful to come, not a word of which they comprehended. Mrs. Lowe smiled to herself and kept out of it. Pretty soon a mountain of clean pots and pans began to stack up. Harold and Roland were discovered playing sardines in the vestry.

Janet Martin and Fuji Nakamura grabbed dishtowels.

"Retta Mae is amazing," said Fuji.

Janet laughed. "You wait," she said, "Retta Mae'll end up adopting those four girls. Old Man Yee will have to send to China for new recruits."

Fuji giggled. The four girls, not understanding one word, smiled. Their oval faces dimpled demurely. They kept right on washing pots and pans.

The sheriff's deputy was checking out the makeshift dispensary with Doc when Larry and Charlene Jepsen found him.

"Ruth's probably gone up to Sacramento," he said. "She probably figures to take advantage of the accidental school holiday."

"Not Ruth," said Charlene. "She wouldn't do that."

"Charlene's right," said Larry. "Something's wrong. I can feel it."

Charlene turned and looked at Larry, amazed, simply amazed. She stood back, speechless, took both his hands in hers and beamed at him. There were tears in her eyes. "Larry Jepsen, I love you," she said finally.

"You do?" The question sort of slipped out. Charlene had been acting so weird lately. This cancer thing, even though it was over and done with, time to move on.

She squeezed both his hands. Tears ran down her cheeks, "Yes, I love you, and I'm going to love you the whole rest of my very long life," she said, and she leaned over and kissed him, right in front of the sheriff's deputy and Doc and the entire population of Two Sloughs.

Larry guessed he'd never understand her.

Charlene's outburst silenced the Social Hall, one of those blinks of an eye when all the suspicions and rumors and whisperings around town seem to melt away, when everybody's heart is caught and held suspended for a fraction of a second.

On the other side of the room, Father Giulio crossed himself.

Before anyone had time to recover, Freddy Noble barged into the Social Hall, his eyes vivid with panic. "Ruth's missing. Where's the sheriff?"

The deputy looked up, "Hi, Freddy. I was about to go check on her. I'll run down to her house in a minute."

"She isn't there. She isn't anywhere. I've been all over town looking for her." Freddy was breathing heavily. "She's stuck at the school. We got to get a boat over there."

"Wait a minute, Freddy. Calm down. Nobody's going out in a boat in the pitch dark. It's too dangerous," the deputy said.

"Then I'll go myself, Goddamn it." Freddy turned on his heels and ran smack into the sheriff, who was just coming in the front door, wet as a drowned muskrat and tired.

"Now wait a...." sputtered the deputy.

"Where you going, Fred?" asked the sheriff.

"I'm going to find Ruth, Carl. I need a boat."

The sheriff looked at Freddy, who was trembling with rage, then over Fred's shoulder at his deputy who was rolling his eyes and making hand signals, "Not tonight you're not."

Freddy took one wild look at the sheriff and decked him. Right in the middle of St. Anthony's Catholic Church Social Hall. A mean left jab that knocked the sheriff flat. The deputy shoved aside two ladies serving spaghetti and ran for Freddy. The women shrieked and scattered, still clutching their spaghetti pots and their bowls of coleslaw. Larry and Charlene rushed for Freddy, too.

The sheriff sat up woozily and waved the deputy off. "I'll handle this," he said. He rubbed his jaw and worked it back and forth. "Freddy, you're not going anywhere tonight." The sheriff got unsteadily to his feet, "If I have to handcuff you to that cook stove over there, I will. I ought to throw you in...." The sheriff had spied Lionel lurking by the door to the Social Hall. He stopped mid-sentence so as not to frighten the boy. "You and I are going to mount a rescue. We're going to get the Coast Guard. We're going to do it right, and we're going to do it at daybreak tomorrow."

"Tomorrow may be too late, Carl. She may be trapped. She may be clinging to a log somewhere, trying to stay afloat. Christ, I can't just sit here and not do anything. Not again, Carl."

Then Carl remembered Molly, Freddy's wife, and the car accident. He remembered Freddy paralyzed with dread, waiting for news, remembered Lionel in his sleepers, sucking his blanket, watching. "No," Carl said. "I'm putting you in charge of this whole operation. But when you find her you've got to be prepared to help her. You need a davit, maybe a winch, tools. If you work like hell, you can be ready by daylight. Lionel, we're taking you over to the Martins so your Dad can do this job of work." He put his arm around the boy's shoulder. "I'm kind of deputizing him."

"And hear this, Freddy," Carl said under his breath, "I'm not letting you out of my sight 'til tomorrow morning, so get used to it. One false move, and I'll handcuff you in the back of my patrol car. I mean it. I got too much on my hands to mess with you."

Carl went out of the Social Hall rubbing his chin, with Lionel on one side of him and Freddy on the other. The deputy watched them go, started to say something, shook his head, then slumped down at one of the long tables. He sighed. "Think I could change my mind?" he asked. "Have some of that spaghetti?"

All through the night Ruth waited for her redwood tree to tremble, to topple over into the dark water. She fought the cold that edged under her skirt, crept up her legs. She clasped her arms around her chest for warmth, but her hands froze. She stuck them back in her pockets, then grabbed a branch again, afraid of dozing off and falling. She prayed for morning.

All through the night Ruth sang to keep her spirits up. "Be kind to your web footed friends," she sang, "for the duck may be somebody's mother." She sang the descant that the flutes had, and the tuba part. She tried "Che Gelida Manina," but it made her even colder and more lonesome. It was a tenor's aria. She went back to "Here's to Luther Burbank." Her taste in music was decidedly odd out here, she reflected. Her friend Ursula Brown would doubtless have a school psychologist's analysis of exactly why she sat perched in a tree singing "Here's to Luther Burbank, wizard of the flowers." Quite logical, Ruth argued. If it hadn't been for Luther Burbank, Ruth might not have a tree to be up in.... Her rear end was getting sore and her legs were going to sleep.

She rubbed her thighs with her left hand. She was afraid to let go of the tree with her right hand. If only morning would come, she thought. Somebody would come rescue her. Rescue her? She needed rescuing, and she needed rescuing pretty darn soon. Rescuing! She who'd always been so fiercely independent, who had never needed anyone, who had always stood on her own two feet.

At some point during the night the wind picked up. She could hear it in the tree. The branches creaked. She felt the cold front blow right through her sopping raincoat. She tightened her wool scarf under her chin. What was the saying? "Wet as a drowned rat?" She shuddered at the thought of drowned rats.

Another high tide must be due soon. When was the last one? Hadn't Carl said 3:00 p.m.? The river would rise, put more stress on the levees. A horrifying thought came to her. What if other levees had broken, too. What if Lambert Island had flooded as well, the island across the river where all the families of Two Sloughs were holed up in the Catholic Church? Dear God, what if it had flooded? Islands often gave way in the Delta in a kind of domino effect. She knew that. What if the town of Two Sloughs was completely washed away? The children!

What if there was nobody left out there to rescue her?

Carl and Freddy dropped Lionel off at the Martin's house and went on over to the Volunteer Firehouse. Carl scribbled three phone numbers on a scratch pad and handed them to Freddy. "Start at the top," he said, "with the Coast Guard. I'll go to work on the rescue equipment and round up some volunteer firemen."

The Coast Guard couldn't send their cutter until morning. It was moored downstream in Rio Vista. The river was running 140,000 cubic feet per second. They'd never make it up to Two Sloughs anyway.

"Then you'll have to send something you can trail up and launch here in town," Freddy insisted. "We got a real emergency on our hands. A school. No telling how many children...."

Carl and Ben Heimann, the Volunteer Fire Chief, both looked up at that remark.

Freddy listened intently, clenching and unclenching his fist on the desk. "Look," he cut in, "the Governor's real hot on this. Seems his niece is missing. She teaches at the school. Also the president of the bank. Shall I give the Governor your number?"

"Damn," muttered Carl, "the Coral Sea'll be steaming into town if Freddy keeps this up." He lowered his voice, "Ben, you got any body bags?"

"Sure," said Ben. He hesitated. "You figure... to need 'em?"

"Don't know," sighed Carl. "That's ugly water out there. I'll tell you I'm gonna need some men strong enough to pin Freddy. We're gonna have to watch him like a hawk."

"Leave that to me," Ben said quietly. I'll call Tony Riccetti, Louie's nephew."

"The Coast Guard'll be here in three hours," Freddy said. "Now what?"

"Now we eat a bologna sandwich and drink a cup of coffee," Ben said, pulling a waxed paper bundle out of his jacket pocket. You'll need your strength."

Freddy took a bite, but he couldn't get it down. He abandoned the sandwich on the desk and began to pace back and forth across the firehouse until Tony Riccetti arrived and suggested softly that it would be kinder to just hit him over the head and get it over with.

"You sure you want him to go with us on this rescue, Carl?" Ben whispered.

"I'm sure I don't. but I can't leave him, Ben. You remember his wife."

A cold sleety rain began to pelt Ruth's face, driven by the wind. Some time before dawn she began to feel less cold, and that worried her. She dug in her pocket for another Lifesaver and looked out through the branches. The sky began to look a lighter gray, but it was a low, mean looking sky, dissolving into rain. The rain and a thin, cold wind riffled the surface of the water, and, as light trickled through the somber clouds, Ruth realized that all she could see, all around her, was water. The levee was too far away to make out clearly without her glasses, but the middle of the island had turned into a wide, wet, overflowing lake. A flock of mud hens floated on it. Panic crept up on her. There was nobody out there. She was alone. Completely and miserably alone. No one even knew she was there.

She started to cry, then swallowed hard. She couldn't cry. She wouldn't cry. Somebody would save her. She took a deep breath. "Oh, what a beautiful morning," she sang at the top of her lungs. But she couldn't stop crying. "Oh, what a beautiful day." The lyrics were drowned in sobs. She thought of Freddy, playing that tune on his harmonica one late afternoon in the drug store. It seemed so long ago. They'd harmonized on "People Will Say...." Tears streamed down her cheeks. Oh, Freddy. The lump in her throat was so huge that she ate another lifesaver. She didn't even notice that it was lime, her favorite flavor.

She heard something, a kind of a buzz, a heavy insect sound. She could see something black swimming toward her. A rat? A beaver? She blinked through her tears. No, much bigger, further away but inching closer, a small boat of some kind... a boat with two short, fat orange figures in it. They were wearing life jackets, and they were heading toward the trees. "Help!" yelled Ruth. "Help!" But they couldn't possibly hear her over the outboard motor.

She sat staring at the boat, willing it to come closer, trying to make out who was in it. The figure in the back of the little boat leaned over and cut the motor. The figure in the front stood up unsteadily and cupped his hands, "Miss Haaarrrrdy."

Lionel? It couldn't be. "Lionel," she said out loud, but she, who had been singing all night at the top of her lungs, became suddenly hoarse. "Lionel!" she called again, but no sound came. "Over here in the redwoods," she croaked. "Lionel!" she tried again. "Over here!" There was very little current now. The water levels must have equalized inside the levee. Lionel pointed toward her tree, then sat down in the boat, put the oars in the oarlocks and began to row toward her.

"Look out for the flag pole," she called. "And there's a tree down beside me."

Jimmy caught one of the branches below her and pulled the boat in toward the trunk.

"Jimmy?" Ruth asked incredulously. "You kids shouldn't be out here. It's dangerous."

"Look who's talking," snorted Lionel.

"Now watch out, Miss Hardy. This boat is real tippy," said Jimmy.

"You're gonna have to lower yourself down easy and step right in the middle," warned Lionel. "Wait 'til Jimmy and me have hold of the tree."

Ruth stared speechlessly down at the two boys.

"O.K., come on," said Lionel, "but watch it."

Ruth eased herself painfully up to a standing position on the wet branch. Her legs were numb with cold. Her feet were scratched and bloody. It looked a long way down.

"Come on," Lionel said sternly. "Concentrate."

Ruth had lost all feeling in her feet. She kept slipping on the branch. She grasped a branch beside her to steady herself; then she couldn't get the fingers of her right hand to unclasp again. She had to peel them up, one finger at a time. "I don't think I can get down," she whimpered.

"You can do anything if you try hard enough," scolded Lionel. "You're not trying."

Oh, God, her own words, thrown back at her. She clenched her teeth and eased herself down, scraping her thigh against the trunk of the tree, breaking branches as she clung for support, feeling for a branch beneath her numb feet. She lowered herself down slowly, trying to feel the balance point on the branch beneath her. Suddenly her foot slid off the branch. She dropped. She hung by one hand, scrambling to get her legs around something, to pull herself back up.

"Forget that branch. There's one below it. More to the left," said Lionel.

"My hand's slipping," gasped Ruth.

"Hang on," yelled Lionel. "No, left. Down more. There."

Ruth clung to the tree, sobbing, shivering.

"If she falls in," muttered Jimmy, "we'll never get her into the boat. She'd tip it over."

"Hang on with both hands," insisted Lionel. "Hard. The next one's easy."

"Wait," she gasped. "I've got to rest."

"Oh, man," muttered Jimmy. "She'll never make it. She can't climb worth a damn."

"Shut up," said Lionel. He called up to Ruth, "Work around to the other side. There's better branches there. Get going."

Ruth had heard Jimmy, and it made her mad. "I can too climb, you little brat," she thought. Some feeling was coming back into her toes. She could get a better grip now. She found one foothold, then another. But it was harder climbing down than up. When she was almost to the water level she worked her way around the trunk again until she was right above the boat. Finally, Ruth reached down until her toes touched the seat of the boat, but as she began to lower herself her feet slipped on the wet seat. She fell over into a heap in the bottom of the boat, rocking it dangerously. Water poured over the rail.

"Watch it," Jimmy yelled, leaning to the high side. "Look, stay still. Put this life jacket on." He began to bail furiously with a coffee can.

"What are you doing out here?" Ruth had felt the boat settle beneath her weight. They had about three inches of freeboard.

"My dad won't let anybody ride with me without a life jacket," Jimmy insisted, continuing to bail.

"Your Dad knows you're out here?" Ruth asked incredulously. Jimmy ducked his head down and kept bailing. Lionel looked uncomfortable.

"Look, Miss Hardy, try to get it on," Lionel said, handing her the life jacket again. "It's kinda rough over by the drug store."

Ruth struggled into the life jacket. She began to shiver violently. "What possessed you to....?"

"Here, we brought you a blanket," Lionel said.

It was one of the old army blankets from Freddy's bedroom. Soaking wet.

Jimmy yanked on the starter cord of the outboard. The motor sputtered and died, and sputtered and died. "It was Lionel's idea," he said grimly.

Ruth huddled under the blanket, but she couldn't stop shivering.

"Lionel was spending the night at my house, and Freddy couldn't find you. Freddy went down to your house, and you weren't there. He couldn't find your car. He went crazy. The sheriff said Freddy couldn't look for you or he'd throw him in jail, and Freddy punched the sheriff." Jimmy pulled once more, and the tiny motor caught. Lionel pushed off. They began to inch away from the tree.

Ruth sat facing backwards toward this sober little boy with his hand on the tiller of his one and a half horsepower outboard motor. She knew she should take charge, assume control. They were in terrible danger. Her weight had lowered the boat until they were nearly sunk in the water to begin with. There were snags and power poles and probably electrical wires and underwater hazards. That other redwood tree was out there somewhere, submerged. She was the school principal, for pity's sake. She sat and shook.

She should at least turn around and keep watch. She swung carefully around until she faced forward and met Lionel Noble face to face. He was studying her.

"You still cold?" he asked.

"But why did you...?"

"I dunno," he said, looking away. "I didn't want you to go and die like my Mom did, and have him be sad all over again." He shrugged his shoulders. "I just didn't want to go through it again."

Ruth sat shivering uncontrollably, staring at the strange freckled face before her. The rowboat inched across the vast expanse of murky water.

"How did you know where to find me?" she asked after a while.

"We figured you'd be worried about the band instruments," Lionel said.

The water got much rougher as they made their way toward the bridge. The rain was coming down hard again. "Jimmy, we should be headed more up that way," Ruth said, pointing.

"No," said Jimmy, "we need to quarter this chop, or we won't get anywhere. I don't think we can make it back across the main channel. We better try for the levee and hope somebody sees us."

At that moment an eddy caught them, swung them sideways. Ruth gripped both rails of the boat. "Look out!" she screamed. The boat veered toward a piece of floating barn.

"Paddle, Lionel," yelled Jimmy.

"I'll row," said Ruth.

"Sit still!" hollered Jimmy behind her.

Ruth sat still.

The boat tipped; the motor coughed; the boat shuddered, held for a moment by the force of the eddy. Lionel got down on his knees in the bottom of the boat and began to stroke powerfully with the paddle. Jimmy revved the one and a half horsepower motor, and the two boys managed to break them free.

But as they neared the levee and the east anchorage of the Two Sloughs Bridge, Ruth could see angry water in the main channel, up nearly to the deck of the bridge, rushing under it, roiling with tree trunks and fence posts. She could see the speed of the water as the rafts of debris barely cleared the bridge. The bridge clung to a little fringe of levee. Jimmy was right. They'd never make it across the main channel. She could make out the shapes of the buildings up on top of the levee: the pharmacy, the bank, the post office, the grocery store. Then she saw the gap just north of the bridge where Ike's.... "Where's Ike's?" She swiveled around, disoriented, dizzy. There was nothing but a choppy dangerous-looking channel where Ike's used to be.

"That's where the second break was," said Lionel. "Don't wiggle."

Ruth pulled the blanket closer around her and prayed, "Dear God, don't let me be the cause of these children's drowning."

It was the crew back at work sandbagging the west anchorage of the bridge on the other side of the river that spotted them. Dan Martin recognized the rowboat and ran for the nearest boat hauled up on the levee. Bud Zolinsky, the beaver trapper, was on the other side before he got it into the water. Louie leapt in with a rope just as they were pushing off from shore. Bud Zolinsky sat next to the outboard motor. The other two men let him. Bud knew more about currents and eddies than anybody in town. They'd be crazy to get in his way. Harvey raced over to the boat dock to get the sheriff and Freddy.

Even with their powerful motor and Bud at the helm, the men were set downstream two hundred yards before Bud could maneuver them through the flotsam and across the main channel. Once inside the flooded island, he had to work his way back up through debris to the boys. Bud cut the motor twenty yards from the rowboat for fear of capsizing it. There were whitecaps on the water now, and the little boat was seriously overloaded. He let Jimmy work his way into him.

Dan knew Bud was doing the right thing, but he couldn't hardly stand it. The rowboat didn't seem to be getting any closer. "Atta boy," Dan whispered to himself. "Slow her down. Way down. "That's it. At an angle. Watch the drift. Don't hurry it." "Okay, cut her, Jimmy," he called out hoarsely.

"Get the kids," said Ruth.

"No," said Lionel. "She can't stand up. We'll hold the boat. You gotta drag her."

"Wait a minute," called Bud.

They all looked up to see a tangle of fence posts and barbed wire bearing down on them.

"Hang on. I got to work around this." Bud started the motor and eased them forward a few yards. An ugly snarl of timber and wire swept past, a drowned chicken caught by a wing on the trailing edge. "O.K." Bud idled the motor.

Dan and Louie reached over to help Ruth, but Ruth waved them off, threw back the blanket. "I'm fine," she said firmly and stood up. But as she reached for the other boat, the rail of Jimmy's boat sank beneath her into the water. Her legs slipped out from under her.

"Grab her!" yelled Jimmy.

The two men grabbed Ruth under the armpits and hauled her into the bigger boat while Lionel and Jimmy leaned frantically over the high side, trying to right the little boat. The boys clambered in after Ruth. Jimmy's boat lay half-submerged beside them.

"I'll cut it loose," said Louie.

"No!" screamed Jimmy, still clinging to the bowline of his precious "Avenger" with the flame orange rub rail.

Bud looked at the boy. "Here," he said handing Louie a bucket, "Bail like hell. Get her two inches higher in the water."

Louie shook his head, but this was no time to argue. He leaned over and went to it like a madman.

"O.K.," said Bud, "Everybody sit down and hang on."

Dan pulled Jimmy tight against his chest, orange life jacket, bow line and all. He hugged him, his words smothered against Jimmy's wet hair, "What the Jesus H. Christ do you think you were doing?"

Louie clamped a hand on Dan's shoulder, "Done a pretty fair job of it, Dan."

Ruth opened her mouth to say something. What? "Leave the kid alone. He saved my life. Don't be so hard on him." But the tears running down Dan's cheeks stopped her. The way he held that child and couldn't let go. The way Jimmy burrowed his head into his father's chest. She sat watching them, speechless, her teeth chattering.

Freddy and the sheriff arrived in the Coast Guard launch just as Bud guided his boat back into the main channel of the river. The Coast Guard officer watched Bud maneuver the boat for a minute and said, "We get near him, we're likely to capsize him. He knows what he's doing. We'll get below him and hope like hell he doesn't need us."

Jimmy's rowboat bobbed behind Bud's boat like a cork. "They ought to cut that dinghy loose," muttered the sheriff. He and Freddy stood clutching the upstream rail, watching Bud ease his way back across the river. They saw him nose around whole trees, dodge whirlpools, avoid debris, gunning the motor to give him way against the current. They willed him into shore with his precious cargo. Bud's boat and the Coast Guard launch pulled up to the levee at the same time. Freddy leapt from the Coast Guard launch before the sheriff could grab hold of him and waded out to catch the bow of Bud's boat. His face was white with fear.

"It's O.K., Dad. I said she wouldn't die."

Freddy clasped his arms around Lionel, then turned and looked at Ruth.

Ruth sank down in the mud, put her hands over her face and burst into tears.

Freddy let go of Lionel and picked her up. "It's O.K., Ruthie," he said. "It's O.K." He put his jacket tightly around her shoulders, brushed her wet curls back off her face. All the while she sobbed and shivered. "What you need is a nice hot bath and an Old Fashioned." She was so short in her bare feet. He kissed her very gently on her nose, on her eyelashes. "Come on, Ruthie. Lionel and I will fix you up." And he and Lionel bundled her off, one on either side of her, leading her to their car.

Across the river from where Ike's Cafe used to be, and Japan Town and the school and the Bank of Thurgood Bream with the Breams still marooned inside and nobody in a hurry to get them out, the men of Two Sloughs stood transfixed, leaning on their shovels, not saying a word. The levee they stood on could have given way at that moment, and they would have been the last people on earth to notice it. Miss Ruth Hardy had found herself a man. That tough-as-old-shoe-leather school marm had succumbed to the gentlest man in town. And that rotten little kid Lionel had fixed them up.